KILLING FAITH

B.J. WOSTER

CHAPTER ONE

**Present Day
Leeds, England**

Father Alastair Fildew walked along the aisles of St. Gregory's, his footfalls echoing, reverberating off the empty pews. The heaviness in his heart weighed deeply on his mind, and the storm blowing outside—cold and damp—far from ministered to his temperament. He was weary, and as he moved to the vestry to await the usual handful of confessors, he again questioned his life—and his faith; something he found himself doing more and more with each passing year; each passing month.

The sound of the rear door opening drew him from his musings and he sighed. That would be Mrs. Woolmer, he thought, glancing at the time. She was early. Then again, she was always early, although this evening she was earlier than usual. He exhaled audibly and moved sluggishly to the confessional, settled on the hard wooden bench, and waited. When the woman began to speak, it didn't take him long to realize that the voice belonged to someone other than Mrs. Woolmer.

Mrs. Woolmer's voice was raspy—both from age and an indulgence in cigarettes. This voice caressed his skin with its youthful sultriness, but beneath the sensual tone was a timidity that reached deep into his soul. He wished the church hadn't voted to remove the transparent screens in the confessionals, in favor of a more private black veil, for he would have loved to see whether the beauty of the voice matched that of the speaker. He forced himself to hear her words and not dwell on the tenor in which she uttered them.

"Father Fildew?" The voice repeated in a timorous whisper, when the father failed to acknowledge her presence immediately. The tone made the father sit up straighter.

"I'm sorry. I'm here, my child. What is it you wish to confess?" Alastair asked in his soothing ministerial way; the tone all priests learn in which to draw people to confession, so as not to drive them away from it. It was another aspect of his duties that had him questioning whether he was meant for this vocation.

"Are you Father Fildew?"

"I am. What have you to confess, my child?"

"I have nothing to confess, Father. I have not come seeking absolution," the woman whispered, sadness and fear issuing with each word spoken. The father's brow knitted in concern, for she sounded young; but not so young as to have committed no transgressions beyond forgiveness; not so young as to think absolution superfluous. Or did she believe her sins unforgivable? He needed to disabuse her of the notion that pardon was not attainable.

"Absolution..." he started, but she cut him off the moment the word left his mouth; the tremor in her voice more prevalent, along with an urgency that drove the timidity away. She didn't want to hear him speak; rather needed to voice what was in her heart.

"Father, please, I don't believe I have much time," she whispered harshly. Were those tears he heard behind the tremors? Whatever had brought this woman to him on this cold, stormy, blustery night had her very distressed indeed. "Whatever I have done in my life, will go with me to my grave. I am not here for me, but for you—and another."

The knit in his brow deepened, "Me? Why me, my child? I'm not certain I understand." He shuddered, not sure if was the result of the constant chill filtering through the stone walls of the old church or whether it was from the tone of the young woman's voice. An Australian accent, he only just noticed.

"Your brother, Father," the woman whispered, the cadence of her speech picking up momentum, borne out of desperate need for him to hear her and to stop interrupting. "You must do something. He's in great danger. I know he is." She sighed heavily when her desperation went unheeded and he persisted in interrupting her thoughts, her revelations. Yes, she realized that she spoke hesitantly, giving him margin to insert his own thoughts, but it was because she felt uncomfortable in approaching a priest to assist in something that could prove deadly to himself. She was also uncertain how to express a danger of which she was barely convinced herself, but if she sat back and waited for certitude then she knew with a deep conviction that Arran would die.

"Perhaps you are mistaken, child," he replied. "I haven't a brother."

"But you do! Please, you must listen to me," the woman insisted. "You need to help him and...bloody hell!"

"I do beg pardon, miss, but if you could avoid swearing..."

A faint thud sounded from the confessional, soft in pitch, but nonetheless deafening—and then all was silent.

"My child, is all okay?"

The sound of the rear door closing drew a moan from his lips. He'd driven her away, and now she may end in Hell because of transgressions he couldn't get her to confess. He sighed heavily. He really wasn't meant for this—not any more.

"Well, there's nothing to be done for it now. Still, there's nothing like a mysterious visitor to remove the dreariness from the day." He shook his head in bemusement, opened the door, and slid off the bench. After a quick glance about to ensure he was alone, he rubbed his bottom vigorously. He disliked sitting on those hard benches, because they always made his bum fall asleep, almost instantaneously. When the tingling in his bottom had dispelled, he returned his musings to the odd confessor. Perhaps her visit had been a practical joke, or perhaps she didn't appreciate people reprimanding her inappropriate language. He glanced at the clock hanging upon the wall. Mrs. Woolmer still had not arrived, but it would not be long before the back door opened and the aged woman came in, carrying the thunderstorm along with her. She always had a million sins to repent, none worth more than a Hail Mary or two, but if it made her feel better to repent that she yelled at her cat, then so be it.

He saw the foot sticking from beneath the door first, and his brow arched in confusion. "Miss? You're still here? Is everything okay?" He could have sworn he heard her depart; heard the back door close behind her.

Yet, here she sat, indicating she hadn't left as he thought; but then who had come or gone? The question in his mind had his gaze scanning the nearby area, the hairs on his arms rising anxiously. Was there another prankster hiding in the shadows; a co-conspirator to the girl sitting silently in his confessional? That would not be a first. Kids who came in, pretending an urgent need to confess their sins, before pulling some prank upon his person and then bolting out the rear door; laughter rumbling from the rafters. They always found themselves so amusing.

Still, she didn't sound like a child, rather a woman of sophisticated speech. Educated. Not a foolish teenaged imp who found wit in winding up a priest. That had him asking himself again—why *was* she still sitting in his confessional in silence? Why had she not spoken since her strange warning?

The only possibility was that she was pouting because he had chastised her, he decided. It certainly would not be the first time he'd had a parishioner go silent because he'd berated them instead of coddled them. Of course, it wasn't his job to berate, rather he was supposed to coddle and encourage, so for him to go against his training...well, it's no wonder so many fell silent, fell out of coming at all. It again had him questioning why he continued to don his collar. Still, his discontent came second to the woman in the confessional. Obviously for her to still be here meant she truly needed his council.

"I apologize for my abrupt manner, my child," he said, taking a tentative step towards the door. "If you wish to continue speaking, I will listen with an open heart and mind, or if you want to sit in contemplation, I will gladly let you do so. You need only let me know you wish me to return. I will be here."

The silence stretched and his brow knitted. He drew in a deep breath, uncertainty bounding about his brain. "Do you need a moment to compose yourself, child?" He tried again, but only silence met his queries. He sighed deeply, knowing that he had but one recourse left him—force her to either speak or leave his confessional. It wasn't a very charitable thing to do, he knew, but he wasn't feeling particularly charitable of late.

He stepped forward, tugged the door open, and found the answer to her silence in the form of a body slumped against the wall. She appeared to be sleeping. *A sleeping beauty,* he thought appreciatively, thinking her voice equaled her fairness after all. With a sharp shake of his head, he dislodged the impious thought from his brain. He leaned over and shook her shoulder gently.

Then he saw the blood.

The hue was a stark contrast to the coloring of her blouse. It seemed alive, creeping towards the outer edges of the material, covering the pureness of white with an evil of red. This was no prank. This woman was dead.

He wondered how this had happened without the slightest utterance of distress. Then he realized her outburst *had* been her distress. "She said bloody hell," he murmured and then crossed himself. He stood and stared at her for a short while, and then the shock began to wear off, and his stomach to protest his macabre need to gape at a corpse. His stomach lurched, and he threw his hand over his mouth. He would not dishonor her death by throwing up on her, that much was certain.

Turning, he crossed himself again and then rushed along the aisle to the vestry. His hands were shaking, his heart pounding in his ears, as he picked up the handset to call the police. Despite the shock, his mind was racing. Who was this woman, and what had her purpose been in declaring his brother in danger, when he did not have a brother? Had she mistaken him for someone else? He did not know of another Father Fildew hereabouts.

Then there was her conviction; the assurance that she needed to warn *him.* It was that assurance that frightened him most.

Someone on the other end of the line answered and he found himself temporarily unable to speak. Why did this woman feel the need to warn him? Who was she, and where had she come from? If he did indeed have a brother, what sort of danger could he be in? Why didn't he know he had a brother?

Hello? 999? Anyone there?

Father Fildew shook the daze clouding his mind and spoke, his voice sounding distant to his own ears, "There's been a murder."

Your name?

"Father Alastair Fildew. St. Gregory's, Seacroft. Please send someone 'round immediately."

He lowered the receiver, the shock at the discovery completely wearing off now. Although he questioned his faith of late and his chosen vocation, he was a priest at present, and accustomed to death—yet this was different somehow. This was murder, and it had taken place inside his church. This murder had taken place while he was speaking to her, beneath his very nose. He certainly wasn't accustomed to that happening.

Still, the woman in his confessional, though she did not think she needed absolution, would assuredly need prayers for her soul. Whoever she was, she did not deserve to die; not like this. There were many questions whirling about in his mind that had no answers. None of this made sense, least of all her declarations about a brother who was supposedly in danger. Even if not his brother, the woman felt convinced that *someone* was in danger—but in danger from who or what? Still those questions were a job for the police to answer.

He moved back toward the confessional with leaden steps and a heavy sigh and his mind drifted to his childhood while he waited for the police to arrive. If he'd meant to be a priest, why was he suddenly questioning his vocation? Was he a priest because of where he was reared? He had been orphaned in infancy; too early to remember his family. He searched his mind, but could recover no image of his mother or his father. His brother? Surely had he a brother, he too would have been at the orphanage. He had never thought to ask the sisters in charge, but he *had* asked after his parents as he had grown. Thinking back now, the answers received had been vague. Had their elusiveness been a way of helping a young boy move forward with his life, or had their intent been to prevent his discovering something about his family that he ought not to know. He had certainly gleaned no insight into his past; did not even know how his parents had died, but they *had* died, and the authorities had sent him to the orphanage. They raised him in their faith—a faith he now questioned as his own. If he was still as confident in his calling as he should be, would the death…

Oh, God, there's a dead woman in there. He shivered, lowering his head into his hands. After a moment, he raised his head, and glanced at the confessional—at the body.

"She's dead, and I'm a priest. At least for now I am."

His gaze fell on the woman again.

Whoever he was, he was a priest at that moment; a priest that someone felt the need to warn. He was a priest for whom an unknown woman died. He moved toward the body and nearly jumped out of his skin when a piercing screech rent the air.

He spun around, closed his eyes, and muttered curses beneath his breath. Mrs. Woolmer had arrived, and her timing was abysmal—as usual.

CHAPTER TWO

Detective Sergeant Melissa Lloyd sat at her desk in the new police station at Seacroft, in Leeds. She missed the ambience of the old station. This new building was a blue monstrosity with sheer glass walls that loomed over her desk and leant a cheery air when the sun shone through—an air that contradicted the oft-times depressing nature of her job. Still, it wasn't for *her* that the new building was constructed, but as a comfort for those who came seeking assistance. After all, when a loved one is murdered, a cheery environment is what they need—or so had been the speculation around the water cooler. None wanted to believe the bureaucrats reasoning that the old building was too old and small to meet the needs of the city.

She had to admit however, that the view from her desk *was* spectacular, especially on rainy nights like tonight. She watched the rain pound against that glass, its rhythm oddly comforting despite the torrential downpour. She would have to make her way home in this in half hour, she thought, glancing at the clock above her on the wall. Still, that was fine by her. She would walk through hellfire itself right now, just so she could get out of here. It had been a long day.

Not that she disliked her work. Far from it, for it provided her with a wide range of stimulation—assault, robbery, battery, mayhem, and murder—the last of which she would like to commit upon her supervisor, CI Wright, she thought, glancing at the man in the office across the room. Her boss seemingly disagreed with the promotion and showed his displeasure almost daily at having a woman sergeant assigned to his unit. Outdated swine, he was. She had met her fair share of chauvinists, starting the day she decided to join the force, but none as blatantly anti-female-police as the current superintendent.

If she didn't love her job as much as she did, she would quit, but since she was certain that quitting would make her boss dance a jig, she stubbornly refused to do so. Not that she *would* quit. He may be a chauvinistic moron, but she was a bloody good detective sergeant, and she would not allow anyone to deny her the pleasure of doing what she loved.

Still, it had been a long day with three breaking-and-entering, five assaults, two domestic disputes, and a mountain of paperwork. Yes, she liked her job, but today she looked forward to getting home, drawing a nice warm bath, luxuriating in the lilac-scented bubbles, while she sipped on a mug of hot cocoa, with a touch of rum. She closed her eyes and allowed her imagination to take flight. In her mind she could feel the bubbles caressing her naked flesh, see her cat, Kookie, sitting precariously on the edge, seemingly as determined as her master for a nice soak. She grinned, imagining Kookie slipping on the wet, slick surface…

"Mel, get in here now!" Chief Inspector Wright yelled, startling Melissa. Her eyes flew open and she jerked, nearly toppling her chair. She muttered death threats beneath her breath, glancing at the five detectives sitting unoccupied at their desks—all of which had clocked in only hours earlier. She however, was supposed to clock out in less than fifteen minutes, so if he was calling her into his office for any other reason than to wish her a good evening…

"What's the hold up, Mel?" His voice boomed. "In here now!"

Melissa stood and made her way through the clutter of desks and filing cabinets, unable to keep the anger from her eyes. He was going to do it. She just knew he was, and if she voiced even the smallest complaint, *he'd* file a complaint.

She no sooner stepped foot into his office when he snapped, "Trouble at St. Gregory's. Get on it!"

He had done it! He had assigned her another case, just minutes before clocking out. Bang goes the hot bath, she thought. If she was lucky, it would not be anything serious and she would be able to close it up and do the paperwork first thing in the morning.

She sighed. Either the CI recognized her talents as a detective sergeant, despite his anti-female stance, and that was why he always called on her at the last minute, or he was determined to drive her insane from lack of rest and the unending paperwork associated with each case file. *It's the latter*, she thought, displeased. Added to her aggravation over the short-notice new case, he still refused to call her Melissa; preferring to shorten her name to the masculine, Mel. It seemed to be his way of accepting her within his unit. Generally, she overlooked the slight. Generally.

"Fine, but next time you call me Mel, I'm not coming in here. My name is Melissa."

"I don't give a shit if you're name is Bob. Get out of my office and over to the crime scene before I have you transferred to the Scottish moors!"

Without a word, she returned to her desk, collected her notepad, bag, and umbrella, and headed for the door. *One day*, she thought, *he is going to retire, or croak at his desk from eating too many sweet treats, and I am going to take his job. That would be poetic justice.* She opened the door and let out a string of curses, as the wind whipped, snatching the umbrella from her grasp.

It was going to be a long night.

CHAPTER THREE

Murder.

Melissa shook her head in dismay as she entered the church—so much for a quick wrap-up and completing the paperwork in the morning.

"Bang goes the bath," she muttered.

The medical examiner had arrived ahead of her and was busily snapping pictures of the corpse—inside the confessional? *Interesting,* she thought.

She stopped and took in her surroundings, a habit she had gotten into early on. She found that if she stood a moment to take stock, she saw something that she might otherwise overlook. Nothing here though. Just the usual array of officers tramping about, a woman crying hysterically against the shoulder of a constable, and a priest sitting on the front pew, his head lowered in his hands. She sucked in a deep breath and then let it out. Time to get to work.

She pulled her notepad and pen from her pocket and headed up the aisle toward the priest. She would not be able to interview the woman until she calmed down anyway. Besides, the priest would most likely provide the best information as he was here more often, and she needed to ascertain his involvement in this if she were going to discover answers. He did not look too good presently, so she knew he'd want to get out of there in all haste. She knew *she* would. Interview him first, she thought, and get him out of the way, and then deal with the hysterical female.

"From your apparent distress," she said softly, settling on the pew, "I take it you're Father Fildew? You called in the report?"

The father nodded, but did not lift his head.

Melissa sighed, "I know this is going to be difficult to relive, Father, but if you could just give me a few minutes to go over what you know happened then perhaps I can let you get home. Maybe have a nice glass of wine to soothe your nerves?" *A lovely Bolney Pinot Noir, like I have waiting on me,* she thought, her resentment mounting towards her super-asinine superintendent for denying her that very comfort.

The priest looked at her then, and her eyes widened in surprise. He was tired to be sure, and his eyes were red and puffy from crying, *but blimey, he's a fair sight to behold*, she thought. She had been without sex too long if a priest was making her daft. Although, she always did find the collar and robe rather sexy on priests; especially attractive priests. She cleared her throat and stopped her mental disrobing of the man. She could always enjoy doing that in her mind later, when she was soaking in that warm lilac-scented bubble bath. In the meantime—back to the business at hand.

"I know this is hard for you, Father, but is there anything at all that you can tell me about this woman? Her name, for instance?"

"I didn't know her."

"Is she not one of your parishioners then?"

"No."

"But you were hearing her confession, or was she dead before..."

"No, she died *during* confession."

"During?" If Melissa needed something to divert her mind away from disrobing a priest, *that* certainly worked.

"Yes, during," Alastair snapped and felt his temper flaring at the memory of it all—the dead woman's vague warning; her utter disrespect for the sanctity of the church with her foul language—her murder.

"Again, I know this is difficult..."

"You have no idea."

Melissa bit back her normally automatic retaliatory remark, because he was right. She witnessed death on a regular basis, but never had she suffered it firsthand. The violence had always been an aftershock, a psychological element for profiling a killer. For her, murder was a word used dispassionately in describing an event— nothing more. Still, she had a job to do and this taciturn priest was her only lead thus far.

"I can't say I understand what you're going through, Father," she started and jerked when he interrupted her.

"Don't *call* me that!" His gaze was blazing when he looked at her again, but as quickly as the fire in his eyes lighted, it died. "I'm sorry. I shouldn't have snapped at you."

"You are a most unusual priest, I must say," Melissa smiled softly. "Never known many of them, but the few I've encountered never seemed to have a temper."

"Not too many of them ever witnessed a murder, I'll wager," Alastair said, smiling sadly. "I'll try to answer your questions now, Detective Sergeant."

"Thank you, Fath...um..."

"My name's Alastair."

"Thank you, Alastair."

"You're welcome..."

"Melissa," she offered.

"You're welcome, Melissa."

"Okay, then, now that we've regained a modicum of control over our emotions, and know by what name to address each other," she said sardonically, "why not we give this another go. You said you didn't know the woman, so let's start with her confession. Did she have time to say anything to you before...well, before she fell silent?"

"She came to warn me that my brother was in danger," the priest offered.

"Ah! Well, that's a good start. What's your brother's name?"

"I haven't a brother," the father said, watching her reaction carefully. The confusion in her eyes mirrored his own. "That was my reaction," he said. "I told her I didn't have a brother, but she was insistent that I hear her out. Only there was nothing to hear. She said that I needed to warn him, cursed, and then fell silent. I thought she left; thought it could have been a prank—a prank in poor taste, but a prank nonetheless. It wasn't though, was it? She sincerely thought I had a brother and that he is in serious danger..."

"Perhaps she had the wrong priest," Melissa interrupted his discourse, for he seriously sounded as if he was on the verge of a mental meltdown.

"That's what I thought too, but she called me by name," Alastair sighed, shaking his head. "I don't know of any other Father Alastair Fildew's around here."

"I'll look into it nevertheless," Melissa said, jotting notes on her pad. "After all, it still could have been a case of mistaken identity. The woman may have thought she was looking for you, but it may have been an Alastair Filman, or another similar sounding name. Letters transposed, unclear speech, sloppy handwriting—all have caused confusion in any number of past incidences.

"Perhaps," Alastair said, sounding unconvinced.

"Is there anything you can add, or recollect, that might help me get a running start on this?" Melissa asked.

Alastair shook his head, "She wasn't here long enough; didn't say enough." He lowered his head into hands and sighed heavily, then looked up suddenly as if recollection slammed into his mind, jarring it. "It didn't register at the time, perhaps because I was dwelling on her voice."

"What didn't register, Alastair?" Melissa prodded when he stopped speaking. He was staring off into space as if trying to recollect precisely what had jarred his thoughts. He blinked again.

"At the time of her death, I heard rustling. Very faint. I thought she was just shifting on her seat. I didn't pay any attention because moving around trying to get comfortable is a common occurrence. I also thought I heard the hinges on the confessional door squeak. That's when I thought she'd given up and left, but there was more rustling and then she swore. It was very faint, as when someone stubs their toe. Then all went quiet again, and…oh God, she was….If only I'd paid closer attention, I would have known there was an assailant…"

"And you could have done nothing had you known," Melissa interjected.

Alastair lowered his head and started weeping quietly.

"I'll leave you alone for a bit." Melissa placed a hand on his shoulder. "You're free to leave at any time. I'll just go speak with the other witness..."

"She's not a witness," Alastair sniffled, wiping his nose. He felt an inexplicable loss when she moved her hand from his shoulder. He shook his head, *another reason to question my faith if I'm having impure thoughts about both a dead woman, and a cop.*

"Pardon?" Melissa asked.

Alastair's head jerked upright, worried he'd spoken that last thought aloud, but her gaze was still professional. He sighed in relief, "Mrs. Woolmer is so distraught because she came upon the body. My fault really. I should have thought to lock the door. She's not a witness," Alastair muttered and then retreated into his misery again. Melissa stood and moved away. He needed his desolation and she needed to search for clues.

Fifteen minutes of examining the body told her nothing more; at least nothing helpful to her investigation. The woman appeared to be in her mid-to-late thirties and was well groomed—professionally so. The faint scent of the latest fashionable perfume, *Fame* by Lady Gaga, drifted into her nostrils as she bent to examine the well-manicured hands closer. There was always hope in a murder investigation, that the victim managed to struggle just enough to collect skin cells beneath the fingernails, or rip off a piece of the offender's clothing or jewelry. She returned the hand carefully as it was found. There appeared to be nothing—at least nothing discernible to the naked eye. In this instance the body lie against the back wall as if in repose. How could someone open the confessional and inflict a death blow without the victim so much as even throwing up her hands to ward off said blow. Yet it appeared as if just that had occurred. The woman's hands lay at her side, unstained by death. If not for the red blotch staining the front of her clothing, the detective sergeant would have thought a tap upon the shoulder would wake the woman. Melissa sighed.

She released the body to the medical examiner, and made her way over to the confessional, but as with the body, nothing stood out. It would be up to the forensic team to suss out any evidence here. She rubbed her temples vigorously, groaning.

Her gaze located Alastair Fildew, still sitting, head lowered in his hands. She couldn't hear him from this distance, but the barely perceptible movements of his shoulders, made her think that he was weeping. Somehow, he was twisted up in what happened here tonight. He swore ignorance as to the identity of the victim; had vowed he'd not seen nor heard anyone come or go, definitively, but, most importantly, his misery was genuine. If he harbored any guilt in life, it was nothing to do with this murder.

She compelled her thoughts to revisit the crime scene, her gaze coming to rest on the small bits of blood puddled on the floor of the confessional; splatters from the knife as it was pulled from the woman's chest, most likely, as it trailed along the floor to just outside the confessional. The abrupt end to the trail told her that the assailant likely wiped the blade before walking away. That much she could discern, but if she could but will that blood to speak, to tell her more than just how it came to be there...her job and life would be a lot easier; although, should her fellow detective sergeants discover her habit of asking the evidence to answer her questions and solve her murder cases, they would probably seek to have her committed. When she finally blinked again, Father Fildew was standing in her periphery, and she jumped, startled.

"If we're going to get to the bottom of this," he said without preamble, his tone hoarse, but determined, "we need to start at the boy's home where I grew up. Kirkstall Lodge. If I had...have...a brother," he amended, "then the information should be in the records there. If the lodge is no longer open, then there is certainly someone, somewhere, who could provide information on where to locate the records for boys residing there in the mid-to-late sixties."

"I thought you said that you didn't have a brother..."

"I don't. Not that I'm aware of."

"How can you be unaware of a sibling, Alastair? Isn't it more likely that the woman simply sought out and informed the wrong Alastair? That would be the simplest explanation, would it not? And while I sympathize with your need to discover if you do have a relation out there, my job isn't to assist in that endeavor; rather it's to locate the killer of the woman sitting dead in your confessional."

Alastair nodded, but something inside him wanted there to be a brother. If there was indeed a brother, then he'd have a sudden purpose in life—to seek out that family and help in whatever predicament that possible brother may be facing. The issue he was facing, was that he didn't have the first clue how to run an investigation of this sort, so he needed to convince this detective sergeant that the brother might provide an invaluable lead.

"While I comprehend that the simplest answers are generally the correct ones, would it not also be prudent," Alastair pressed, "to follow all leads in order to eliminate all possibilities rather than to make an assumption that may prove false? What harm could there be, after all, in finding out whether I have a relation out there. If not, no harm has been done; if so, then we can assume that this woman had the correct individual and locating my brother may lead us to this woman's killer..."

"I get your point. What was the name of the boy's home again?"

"Kirkstall Lodge."

Melissa jotted down the name of the boy's home, and then set about disabusing Alastair over his role in this mess, "I think you need to understand that there is no *we*, Alastair," she added, although her mind conjured all sorts of things they could do as *we;* the only practical, and least satisfying of which, was to converse.

"We? I don't follow..."

"You said, a few minutes ago, just before you started on your attempt at persuasion, that if *we're* going to get at the bottom of this, but I'm here to tell you that there is no *we*; however, *I* will do all *I* can to find this woman's murderer and if, in the course of that investigation, I discover you have a brother, I will be certain to let you know. I know you somehow feel responsible for this young woman, and that you would like to know if you truly have a brother out there somewhere, but this is an open police investigation, and you're a priest, not a cop."

"I need to go with you," Alastair declared passionately. "That young woman died trying to relay information to me about a brother that I don't know anything about, but who could be in serious danger. It stands to reason that if we find him, we find answers."

"So you've said, but it may not even be your brother at all. You don't know for certain that she even got the right person, and while I understand your need to find answers, that's what I'm here for—to provide you with those answers," Melissa said with her twentieth sigh for the evening. "Surely you can appreciate that allowing a civilian to accompany me on my investigation could cost me my job, and I happen to like my job."

Alastair's shoulders drooped; his countenance a portrait of despondency.

She placed a hand in comfort on his arm. "I promise you, that if I discover that you have a brother, you'll be the first to know," Melissa whispered, "and I will do what I can to find out why this woman was murdered in an attempt to warn you about him. However—and this is a big but—in order for me to do my job, I need you to trust me unreservedly; and more than anything, I need you to go home and stay out of my way."

"I trust you," Alastair said softly, but it didn't slip past Melissa that he hadn't agreed to stay out of her way. She heard yet another sigh slip past her lips and suddenly longed for that bubble bath and a hot tottie with an extra splash of Bourbon. She'd long forgotten about the hot cocoa with rum, or the bottle of wine. Neither would be strong enough to ward off the weariness of the day.

"If you get in my way, Alastair, you know I have the authority to lock you away in a cell for the duration of this investigation."

Alastair lifted his head and the anger simmering in his eyes took Melissa by surprise. *There is definitely more to this man than meets the eye,* she thought. Weren't priests supposed to have doe-eyes, be mild-mannered, and incapable of losing their temper? Not that she would know, she wasn't Catholic. Maybe she'd seen too many priests stereotyped in movies; maybe they actually *did* have tempers. This one certainly seemed to.

"You do what you need to do, Detective Sergeant," he whispered with far more confidence than he felt, "and I'll stay out your way."

"But not out of my investigation," Melissa added.

Alastair stood there a moment longer, his gaze boring into hers. He hadn't a clue what needed doing and could really use her help, but if he needed to go it alone, he'd take it one step at a time. He stared at her a moment longer and then turned and left the church.

"Damnable priest."

After a moment, she collected her wits, and her gear, and left. She had a trip to make early tomorrow morning. She needed to follow up on her only lead, and prayed that it actually led somewhere. Tonight however, she was going to take that bloody bath she'd been denied. She needed a good soak, but more than anything she needed to get her mind focused on this investigation and her hormones firmly in check. Priest or not, she found him incredibly potent. She sighed as her mind did return to the investigation. As much as she hated to admit it, Alastair had given her the only potential lead in this investigation—this mysterious brother. At least until the medical examiner came back with his findings. If the death of this woman was directly related to another person, then finding that person may provide the answers she needed to solve this case.

CHAPTER FOUR

Melissa pulled into the drive of Kirkstall Lodge at six o'clock the following morning. As she climbed the steps, she admired the antiquated multi-story brick structure and the well-kept grounds before moving to rap on the front door. An elderly man answered the knock and immediately ushered her into a nondescript antechamber. He told her to wait—so, she took a seat and waited.

As six-thirty came and went, her impatience mounted, and the swaying of her foot increased its momentum. With a frustrated sigh, she uncrossed her legs, slamming her heel loudly onto the floor, the sound echoing off the walls of the empty corridor.

She yanked her satchel from the bench beside her, pulled it onto her lap, and then reached inside to retrieve her laptop. Perhaps she could occupy her time better while she waited, she thought, depressing the start button. She clicked on Internet Explorer, thankful that the old building had a WiFi signal she could access without need of a password.

She typed in the homepage for Google, and then typed "Alastair Fildew". She had no justifiable reason for performing a search on the priest, other than an innate curiosity; however, a moment later, she clicked the laptop closed and slid it back into her satchel. There was not a single listing for him, not even a blurb about his being a priest. He had left not a single footprint during his adulthood, at least nothing that came up on Google. Not easy to do in this technological age.

Next, she slid her mobile phone from her coat pocket and dialed the medical examiner's office. The desk clerk put her through immediately.

"Had time yet to give me a cause of death?" She asked without preamble.

Single stab wound. Pierced the heart. Nicked the rib cage and punctured the lung, so the person who stabbed her was probably a professional. It isn't as easy to stab someone successfully in the heart as some people might think. Especially with this level of accuracy. Too many bones, muscles, and other barriers. Yet this person knew precisely what type of weapon is best, although I haven't a precise blade yet. Thrusting into the heart is easiest using a double-edged knife with the blade held horizontally and aiming to the left of the target's sternum.

"Always good to know. I appreciate the update. How long before we get something back on her fingerprints?"

Couple of days. Have a backlog, you know? I just happened to notice the wound and took a quick look. Not very many professional hits come through this office, if you know what I mean.

"Apparently, and I don't have professional hits fall into my lap every day either. Keep me posted."

Will do.

The connection broke and Melissa stood, pacing the room. Did the medical examiner just indicate that this wasn't a run of the mill murder, but a professional hit? And one that had been inadvertently handed to her by her foolish superior officer. Would he yank it away from her when he discovered it was more than just a gang killing, a lover's quarrel turned ugly, or some other idiotic retribution-type slaying? In all her years with the police, she'd never even thought that there would be a professional hitman traversing the streets of Leeds; would never have crossed her mind that she'd ever be investigating one such as this. Yet the medical examiner had plainly indicated, although without confirmation as yet, that only someone with skill could have killed in this manner.

Her thoughts were cut short when the door opened and a priest motioned for her to follow.

Melissa's heels clicked and echoed loudly as she followed the father down first one corridor and then another. She glanced about her at the uniformed boys standing in a queue along one wall, their faces somber. She didn't know where they were headed, but they certainly didn't look pleased about going.

"Children should be happy," she whispered to herself, not realizing just how loudly she'd spoken until the father in front of her replied.

"Find them a family that will take them in, care for them, and love them for who they are—and they will be. We're here." He opened a door, and then stepped aside, allowing Melissa to pass.

An aged man stood from behind a large oak desk and came around to greet Melissa. "I am Father Nicholas. What brings you to see me, Detective Sergeant?" He waved to a chair in front of his desk, indicating that Melissa take a seat. When Melissa complied with the silent command, the father moved back to his own chair.

"I'm investigating a murder that took place at St. Gregory's, in Leeds, last evening."

"That's interesting. It's a bit of a jaunt to come for an investigation, unless perhaps you suspect one of our boys?"

"No, Father, of course not. I was merely hoping you could tell me about the priest that presides there. I understand he was an orphan and resided here in his youth."

"Father Alastair Fildew," Father Nicholas nodded, reaching for a file on the side of his desk.

"Yes," Melissa said, her brows knitting. "You've kept in touch with him over the years, I see."

"Although I do attempt to remain in contact with all of the boys that pass through this home, Alastair didn't seem inclined to do so. No, he came to see me late last night. If not for his connection to the church and to Kirkstall, I would have insisted he come back today; especially since he woke me from a very nice sleep. And now I'm going to make a huge assumptive leap that you're here for the same information he was."

"Yes I am, Father," Melissa said tightly.

"Anger at him is a waste of energy, as it cannot undo what's already been done. It isn't my place to lecture you, Detective Sergeant, but if you had a brother unknown to you, you'd take steps to locate him also."

"If I were in his position, I'd let the police do their job, as I was told to do," Melissa retorted.

"I've only just met you, dear lady, but I have sincere doubts as to the veracity of that statement." The father grinned at her chagrin. "Now, tell me what you need to know. Thanks to the changes in the laws, our records are public and I can give you as much detail as is available to me."

"Well, I guess by your earlier response, that Alastair actually does have a brother?"

"Indeed," the father replied, glancing down at the file.

Melissa shook her head in wonder, "Wow."

"Why wow?"

"I just didn't give it much credence, to be frank. I sincerely believed this would be a dead end; just something I could do to bide my time until the medical examiner gave me a real lead." She shook her head in embarrassment and then reached into her satchel for a pen and pad.

"It is easier to dismiss something out of hand, than it is to work to find the truth."

"Sounds like something you tell people who've lost their faith in God."

Father Nicholas smiled his reply and then returned the subject to the reason for her visit, "What can I tell you, Detective Sergeant?"

"Well, if Alastair had a brother, I could use the name, and where I can find him," Melissa said, pulling a pen from her satchel. "If that information is in the file, that is."

"It is, to some extent." The father started flipping through the pages of the file, "Are you at all familiar with a program that took place in the sixties known as the £10 POM Program[1]?" He asked, as his fingers, arthritic with age, slowly flipped through page after page.

"No, I can't say that I am."

"When were you born?" He asked, finalizing his search. He laid the file open on his desk and waited for her response. Melissa wanted

---

[1] There is more to this program than just the adoption of British children. For more information on the £10 POM Program (10-pound pom) visit: http://tenpoundpom.com/pages.php?pageid=86 (current as of 2012)

to ask him simply to impart the information; that she wasn't there for a history lecture, but pushed her impatience aside.

"I was born in 1980."

"Then you would not have been affected by the program, but Alastair and his brother were," he looked down at the page, his finger tracing downward to the information he sought, "Arran, was his name."

"I'm not sure I understand what the program has to do with my investigation."

"I'll explain," the father said, and then settled back against his seat. "In the sixties, the British Government had this brilliant notion to send orphans to live with families in Australia."

"Australia!"

"That's the same reaction that many British citizens had when the media released news of this program some time back. You must not watch the tele much."

"And you do?"

"No, but I do read the newspaper."

"So, Alastair and his brother…" Melissa started, only to have Father Nicholas anticipate and interrupt her.

"No, only Arran. Many family units were ripped apart during that time. Some siblings remained in orphanages here in England, while the government transported some to new families in Australia. Alastair remained here. Why that is, I cannot tell you. Perhaps the family could only take in one infant."

"Infant? So, that would explain why he didn't know he had a brother. They were separated near birth."

"Stands to reason."

"With the government restrictions lifted on this information, almost anyone who knew where to look would know of this program."

"And you want to know if anyone else has come asking after Alastair?" The father asked intuitively. "Or perhaps his brother?"

"Yes, actually, but I'd also like the names of the adoptive parents in Australia. Is that information in the file?"

"I'm afraid not, but if you wish to know anything further about the children fostered out to families in Australia, you can go search out the records at Australia House. Just inquire into the £10 POM Program and they should be, possibly, able to provide you information on the family and where they lived." Melissa continued scribbling in her notepad as the father continued to talk. "As for any other inquiries, there was a young woman here a few days ago asking after Alastair, and now you and Alastair have come asking after Arran." The father stopped short of asking what was going on as any other normal citizen might, although there was a curiosity in his tone. Melissa chose not to enlighten him.

"Do you remember the woman's name?"

"I'm afraid I don't remember. Old age plays havoc with one's mind."

"Perhaps a description?"

"Ah, now *that* I do remember. My mind may be going, but my eyesight is still good enough to appreciate a beautiful woman." The priest winked, and Melissa shook her head in bemusement. Men, it seemed, were the same whether they wore a collar or not, and no matter their age.

She arched her brow, and lifted her pen deliberately in preparation to write. The priest caught the clue and launched into a very thorough description; a description that was spot on to the victim. That told Melissa the woman had not made a mistake in her identity of Alastair Fildew, and that Alastair did indeed have a brother, whose life could very well be in danger.

She finalized her notes, and then stood to leave, "I appreciate your time very much," Melissa said, moving toward the office door.

"May I ask what you intend to do about Alastair?" Father Nicholas inquired, remaining seated at his desk. "He's been distressed greatly over these turn of events and needs understanding and compassion, not wrath."

"You make it sound as if I'm going to beat him over the head with a club when I next see him."

"Aren't you?"

Melissa shook her head and sighed, "I hadn't really thought about what to do. I just know he cannot be allowed to interfere in a police investigation, no matter his motivations."

"Just remember what I said, and don't do anything rash."

"Like throw him jail?"

"Or hit him over the head with your club," the father rejoined.

Melissa snorted, "I'll try to remember his upset and not do anything rash. Thank you again for your assistance, Father."

"You're more than welcome. If you need anything else, you know where to find me. Just impart to Alastair that, should *he* need me further, he is to wait until a civilized time. If he ever awakens me from my sleep again, *I* may just crack him over the head with a club."

Melissa laughed, and pulled the door closed on her way out. Alastair had been right about coming here. This visit had afforded her much-needed information in which to keep the investigation moving ahead. Without this visit, her investigation could very well have stalled early on. She reluctantly decided to thank him for his assistance, but still needed to warn him off interfering further. After all, he'd discovered that which he needed to know—he had a brother.

She needed to get back to Leeds quickly before he went chasing after that brother. Since they now knew his brother was tangled up in the death of the woman at the church, and could very well be in danger also, Alastair may end up getting into more mischief than from which he could extricate himself.

CHAPTER FIVE

One Month Prior
Perth, Western Australia

"Arran?"

Arran Masters stood on the balcony in his twentieth-floor apartment, overlooking Swan River. It was because of the view that he chose to live in this area of Perth, even though his job as Chief Financial Officer for S&W Renewable Energy meant he spent more time on the road than enjoying this view.

"Arran, are you listening to me?"

He was, but he wasn't. His mind was on everything that had happened over the past week. His life had just taken a drastic turn and put him on a road that he must travel alone, but how to tell Jane?

He wished that she'd chosen not to come over this evening, but there was generally no stopping Jane. If she felt something wasn't right, she didn't rest until she sorted it through. It was the reporter in her, he supposed. That propensity to uncover truths worried him greatly, because she perceived something off about him, and she was determined to have it out. Unfortunately, for her, he was just as determined not to let it out. The urgency in her voice finally penetrated the fog enshrouding his brain and he turned to face her.

"Why weren't you listening to me, Arran? What is wrong with you lately? You haven't been the same for days now."

With a gaze filled with sadness, he lifted his hands and placed them on either side of Jane's face; then leaned down and kissed her tenderly. Jane gasped against his mouth. It was a kiss of farewell, and she knew it. She'd been the recipient of that sort of kiss several times in her life; had even been the bearer of a breakup kiss on occasion.

When he lifted his lips and moved to draw her into his embrace, Jane took a step back.

"You bleedin' twat. I've given you five years of my life, and you're dumping me, aren't you?"

"Come, sit with me," he said softly, drawing her into the living area. He settled onto the sofa and pulled her down to sit beside him.

"I've been given more responsibilities at work that are going to keep me far too busy for a relationship. I'm simply not going to have time…"

"Don't, Arran! Just don't!" Jane snapped, jumping up.

"Don't what, Jane?" Arran asked, pretending ignorance. It was a poor job of acting too, if Jane's outburst was any indication.

"Don't treat me like I haven't a brain and can't reason; like I haven't good enough eyesight to see when a load of dung is being dumped on me. I'm not stupid, Arran! I don't know what's going on here, but I can see in your eyes that you're in trouble…"

"And now you don't know what *you're* talking about!" Arran interrupted. "Let's just call it what it was and be done with it, okay? We had a good time together, but now it's over."

"You sodding wanker! If you expect me to believe that I was nothing more to you than a good five-year lay…"

"Yeah, you *were* good," Arran said callously. The hand that snaked out and slapped him across the face snapped his head sideways. He rubbed his cheek and watched as Jane stormed for the front door.

"I'll have your things taken 'round to your mums," he called after her and heard her cry of outrage as she yanked open the door. "And give my regards to Alastair, will you?"

He saw her stumble, but willed her to keep walking. She didn't look back as she reached for the doorknob and slammed it closed behind her, shaking the door in the jamb. "I love you, Jane," Arran whispered, bowing his head.

"You didn't have to give her the boot, you know," a man said, stepping from the bedroom. "I know if that was my woman, I'd think twice…"

"Well it wasn't your woman, and it was my decision, so leave it alone. I don't need her mixed up in this business."

"Speaking of business, Mr. Rudd asked that I bring you in to discuss the terms of your new business arrangement."

Arran snorted, shaking his head. "What possible terms could there be? Thanks to my excellent bookkeeping skills, I discovered S&W is a money laundering enterprise, so I either allow him to twist my arm into acquiescence of his new terms, or he disposes of my now-former fiancé—and, possibly, myself. No tough decision there. Why didn't he just kill me?" The question was rhetorical, but Rudd's enforcer answered anyway.

"Perhaps he loves you. Hell, I don't know, and I don't care. How you and the boss came to your current arrangements isn't any concern of mine. I was just sent to fetch you for your meeting; and since you have a good idea of what's expected, it should be a fairly short meeting."

"Let's just get out of here," Arran snapped, snatching up his leather jacket and heading for the door.

****

Jane sat in her car, tears of anger and anguish streaming down her face. She was still reeling over what had happened, and her mind was in turmoil. Something simply was not right. It wasn't like Arran to treat her so cold or heartless, and she couldn't believe that he would hurt her this way or that he'd dump her. They talked marriage only last month. They were happy. Then something happened a little over a week ago that changed all of that; changed Arran.

She pulled a Kleenex from her handbag and dabbed the tears from her eyes. Despite her upset, her curiosity over his parting statement was almost too much for her to ignore. Who was Alastair and why would she need to give him regards?

A vague memory tugged deep in the recesses of her mind and a conversation she'd had with Arran a few months ago flittered to the forefront. Arran said that he'd done one of those mail-in DNA tests which revealed he had a relation somewhere in England that he'd hired an investigator to locate. Wasn't it a brother? Didn't he say that relative's name was Alastair?

She wasn't aware of any other Alastair of mutual acquaintance, and certainly not any whom she'd want to give regards to after Arran discarded her unceremoniously.

A movement near the front of the apartment building caught her attention. Arran was leaving, and he looked even more miserable than he did when she'd been arguing with him.

"What are you doing with one of Amherst Rudd's thugs? Oh Arran, what have you gotten yourself involved in, and why couldn't you trust me enough to stay with you and help you through it? Well, you may have quit on me, but I refuse to quit on you. I'm going to find out what you've gotten yourself mixed up in and I'm going to find a way to help you get out of it, starting with a visit to your parents. If you won't help me, then maybe I can convince your brother to help me help you."

****

"From the conversation I overheard, Arran thought it best to get rid of his long-term relationship; but instead of leaving, she's sitting in her car, watching the building," a man bearing the likeness of a walking Pit Bull said into a mobile phone. "What do you want us to do?"

I need to be certain that she doesn't know anything. Follow her closely, and keep me informed of her activities. He may think he's done her a favor by getting rid of her, but that doesn't mean she's ignorant of things; and since she's a reporter, so she may prove a nuisance. If she starts pointing her nose in our direction, we may have to cut it off.

CHAPTER SIX

**Present Day
Leeds, England**

"Harry," Melissa said into her mobile, "I need an address for a Father Alastair Fildew."

Did you say Father, *Mel?*

"That's right, Harry, and I will ask again that you not call me Mel. Just because that jackass..."

Whoa, slow down, Melissa. I got the message.

"Yeah, well it took you too long to get the message, so do you have an address or don't you?" Melissa snapped, carefully maneuvering through traffic as she entered Leeds. "Father Alastair Fildew. He's the priest at St. Gregory's."

Have you checked the church?

"After what's happened, I don't think he'd go back there," Melissa said, blowing her horn when a motorist cut dangerously close to her bumper.

Well, if you suspect him of being at home, he would. Most Fathers I know reside on church grounds.

"Oh! I didn't know that," Melissa said, turning at the next street heading toward St. Gregory's.

That's okay, Mel...I mean, Melissa, Harry corrected quickly, and Melissa knew he was grinning at her, *not all of us can be perfect little Catholics.*

"I'm not Catholic at all," Melissa retorted. She punched the end call icon on the mobile and tossed it onto the seat beside her. She depressed the accelerator and shot through traffic, relying on her siren and flashing lights to get her there in one piece. She had to catch Alastair; had to get there before he took off to God knew where and ended the same as the woman in his confessional. Admittedly, she didn't *know* his intentions. He could be happily meditating or reading his Bible, content with merely finding out his brother's name. He could very well be willing to turn over the investigation to her fully now, and go back to leading little lost sheep.

He could be, but if her first encounter with him were any indicator, he wouldn't be. He would be planning his next strategy on how to find his brother to keep him safe.

Her tires squealed as she turned into the church's courtyard. The moment the car stopped, she rammed it into park, leapt out, and ran up the front steps of the church. He had a day on her investigation, and she couldn't waste time on slow-stepping it through the church, or he could very well slink out the back, and pursue his next clue—if he hadn't left to do so already. She sighed as she peered in one door after another.

If he remained one-step ahead of her in this, she could end up spending the entire investigation hunting him down. It certainly wouldn't help her reputation, if she spent the whole time chasing after him and him solving the crime for her.

Her ire at his interference intensified, and she nearly yanked the next door off its hinges. As it was, it appeared she'd located the door to his quarters, but he wasn't there. She was livid. She knew that wherever he'd gotten off to, it was as a direct result of his conversation with Father Nicholas late last night.

"I have no choice but to await him here, otherwise, he'll jump on the next clue he gets and remain a step ahead of me the whole way. Damnable priest doesn't know what he's doing. If this business proves dangerous, the bastard could get himself in loads of trouble."

She flopped heavily onto the mattress and winced. The mattress was too thin and she felt every spring jam into her bum. She stood and rubbed her bottom, then decided she'd wait for him sitting in the only chair in the room, which she moved to the window. She didn't know precisely where he went or how long she'd have to wait, but until the M.E. concluded his exam, she didn't have anywhere else to be.

"Damnable priest."

CHAPTER SEVEN

It was well into the middle of the afternoon, a good seven hours after her arrival at the church, when Alastair returned. Waiting on him that long, with no more than a power bar for lunch and a bottle of water she'd found in his refrigerator, had her at the height of anger.

He didn't immediately see her sitting next to the window when he entered the room and dropped onto the bed, so she took advantage of being unseen to gain control of her fury, because what she really wanted to do was walk across the room and strangle him. Instead, she drew in a deep breath to reduce her racing pulse, then stood and leaned nonchalant against the wall. She blanked out all expression from her face to prevent his seeing her relief at having located him.

"Where have you been, Father?" Melissa asked, and smiled wide when he leapt off the bed startled.

"When did you get here?"

"I've been here all day, awaiting your return." She reply issued through tight lips which demonstrated to Alastair just how angry she was, and just how hard she was working to restrain that fury. He sighed heavily.

"Actually, I just arrived. I flew in from London a little bit ago."

When she arched a brow in irritation at his confession, he raised his chin, defying her to chastise him. She didn't. Instead, she pushed away from the wall and moved to stand closer, staring at the lines creasing his eyes.

"You look tired, but I guess you would be since you've been busily running my investigation all night."

Alastair moved around her and headed for the small refrigerator, "Yes, I've been busy all night—trying to locate my brother. Can I get you something to drink, Melissa, and try to remember that I asked you not to call me Father. My name's Alastair."

"I remember, Alastair, but calling you Father is my way of reminding myself that you are a naïve priest, unfamiliar with the ways of the world, and unfamiliar with the laws regarding interfering with a police investigation. It reminds me that I should take all of that into account, so I don't assault you, place you in shackles, and stick you in a cell with men who would teach you the ways of the world in a way you wouldn't soon forget. Knowing you're a priest calms me down. So, I'll take a bottle of water," she responded casually, knowing that he only had water to drink.

"All I *have* is water." Alastair replied and she grinned. He reached in and retrieved two bottles of Evian, tossing one at her.

"So what were you doing in London?" She asked, returning to the chair next to the window.

"I needed to go to Australia House to get some information." He saw the storm clouds building in her gaze, shrugged, and settled back onto the bed.

"The information you're looking for wouldn't happen to be about your brother, Arran, would it?"

Surprise registered in Alastair's eyes, but the tired defeat from a moment earlier quickly replaced the surprise. "I see you've been to the boy's home, as I suggested."

"And I see you didn't listen to what I said about staying out of my investigation."

"I couldn't be certain that you would follow up on the lead I provided, and I had to find out if I really had a brother."

Melissa sighed. "It was a good lead, Alastair, and I'm certain that whatever information you located at Australia House will also prove beneficial, but what I can't seem to get across to you is that you're playing with fire."

"I have to find my brother. I have to help him," Alastair said, his tone pleading with her to understand. She refused.

"And what exactly are you going to do once you locate him?" Melissa asked, trying to keep her temper in check. "Because if he *is* somehow mixed up in something that got a woman killed, you certainly are not trained to help him in any way; unless there is more to you than just a black robe and a white collar. Is there, Alastair? Is there something in your background that I'm unaware of that has prepared you to take on crime in this country? A black belt in Jujitsu perhaps? An online coppers correspondence course that you aced?"

"I'm not staying in this country. I have every intention of booking the first flight out for Australia."

"And if I decide to lock your ass in jail instead?" Melissa asked, moving to stand between Alastair and the bedroom door.

"That's your prerogative, I suppose, but you really haven't got a legal reason to do so. For all you know, I'm just going on vacation..."

"You know that's shite and I know that's shite."

He arched a brow at her language, but decided to ignore it. "I have every right to go wherever I please to visit whomever I please. You can't stop me doing that," Alastair refused to be dissuaded or intimidated. She was right that he didn't have the necessary skills should trouble find him; but he perhaps could lend support if his brother truly was in danger.

Melissa stood there shaking her head and sighing repeatedly. What was she to do about this man? He was right that she couldn't detain him from seeking out a relative, but didn't he realize that she'd feel responsible should anything happen to him because she didn't prevent his going?

"Give me time to ascertain whether your brother has a connection to the dead woman?"

"No, because we both already know there *is* a connection. The dead woman told me so; told me that my brother was in danger."

"And you discovered his whereabouts at Australia House?"

"I discovered that he was fostered out to Timothy and Barbara Masters."

"And you think that if we go to Australia, we can help him get out of danger?"

"That's my intent, but you said *we*. I seem to recall yesterday that you said there was no *we*."

"I did and I am fully aware of what I said yesterday, Alastair. I am also fully aware that you're likely going to Australia whether I go or not. I also know that, if that's where the murder investigation leads me, then that's where it leads me. I just have to convince my superintendent that Australia is the only viable avenue open in closing this murder investigation. Chances are he will expect me to conduct interviews over the phone; however, if he concedes, we can fly out tomorrow. Will you give me that much time, at least? Promise not to go flying off half-cocked to Down Under? Let me clear the trip with my CI and contact the local constables in Australia so I can gain their assistance? I can't stop you going, but if we're together, then perhaps I can stop you getting killed."

Alastair nodded, "Thank you, Melissa."

"Don't thank me, Alastair. I still am not certain that it's a good idea for you to go with me, but it's better than having you go alone. At least this way, I can keep you close by if danger rears its ugly head. Have you cleared a vacation with your superiors?"

"I took a leave of absence immediately after the woman in the confessional was murdered. They understood the necessity and are sending a replacement to arrive in time for Sunday mass."

"And how is a priest supposed to afford a ticket to Australia? I certainly can't afford to buy you one, and I can't justify it on my expense account."

"I wasn't always a priest. We're supposed to dispose of all worldly goods, but I just couldn't let go of my savings at the local bank." Alastair blushed sheepishly and Melissa laughed.

"Well, we can't all be perfect little Catholics," she parroted, and downed the remainder of her water. "Don't book your flight until we've cleared everything. Once done, I'll swing by and we'll book them together. That way we're on the same flight."

"I appreciate it, Melissa."

"Appreciate me when this is all done. If you're still alive."

She tossed her empty bottle in the recycle bin and left him to mull over his possible demise.

CHAPTER EIGHT

"The fingerprints came back as those belonging to Jane Chaffin, a reporter in Australia. Flight information has her arrival in Leeds a few days before her death. We know that she was searching for information related to Alastair Fildew, the father at St. Gregory's. He's the one who called in her murder. We also know that she died imparting information to Father Fildew about a brother that the father was unaware existed. This brother, she stated, shortly before being stabbed, was in serious danger."

"You've told me nothing that would justify you getting on a plane," Chief Inspector Wright stated, his demeanor irritated at having her barge into his office with unreasonable requests. "If the brother is in danger, transmit his information to the police in Australia and let them handle it."

"Her murder took place in our jurisdiction, and we have an obligation to…"

"We can find that out using the telephone. It's far less costly."

Melissa sighed and turned to the next page of her notes. She had to keep trying to persuade him, "I also did a check on passengers flying in and out of Australia around the time of Jane Chaffin's death. One name popped. Lachlan Dunne. He flew in the morning after Jane Chaffin, and flew out the morning after her death. I did some research, and he's got a criminal record going back decades. He is purportedly the hired hit man of one Amherst Rudd."

That snared her superior's attention, though she didn't know why, "Did you say Amherst Rudd?" He asked, sitting upright in his chair.

"That's what the investigation turned up. Why? Who's Amherst Rudd?"

"A slippery eel who enjoys torturing those he perceives as threats before eliminating them. He's pretty good at disposing of their bodies too because we have yet to find anything that can link him since no bodies are ever found. Another reason we haven't gotten anything to stick is because he allegedly takes on multiple apprentices and trains them in his methods. This makes it more difficult to pin that particular signature to one person if you have more than one perp using the same MO," Chief Inspector scoffed. "The only reason we know anything at all about Rudd is because of information gained during the interrogation of a famed hit man. Do you remember the case in America quite a few years back, related to a mafia hitman named Charles Carneglia, who purportedly used acid as a torture method for mob bosses such as Gotti and Gambino?[2]

"Rings a bell."

"Well, during his trial, Carneglia told a reporter that he learned the use of acid from Amherst Rudd. Unlike Rudd, he would just threaten to dunk the intended victim into a vat full of the stuff if not told everything but Carneglia said that Rudd would take his time, slowly trickling acid on the person's body to get him to spill his guts, reveling in their pain. Once he'd gleaned all he needed, then and only then would he dispose of the person by suspending them over a vat of acid. The person would be lowered slowly into vat, feet first, until full submerged. Sadistic son-of-a-bitch."

"Sounds as if that would be enough to arrest him? So then why isn't he behind bars?"

"Circumstantial. Supposition. You name a legal loophole, and Rudd has found a way to jump through it. Besides, as I said, eliminating the body means nothing to tie Rudd to the crime—and acid is a good way of getting rid of evidence; and since no one dares come forward to testify against Rudd, the Australian authorities have no way to touch him, not that many of them would. There are rumors that he's bought off or threatened into submission a majority, if not all, of the police."

"What about Carneglia? He obviously is aware of Rudd's techniques, and since he's already in jail, he hasn't anything to lose..."

---

[2] For information on this case from 2009, and other mafia related information, visit
http://www.mafia-news.com/judges-fair-trial-acid-test/#more-1155

"Carneglia denied the reporters account. Said he would never break the omertà[3]. Besides, Rudd's never been associated with any crime on American soil, so it wouldn't matter what Carneglia attested to; however, you saying you've something that ties Rudd to a murder on British soil we can maybe work with. Are you a hundred percent certain of your facts?"

"I'm certain about the data I collected related to Lachlan Dunne and his arrival and departure from England, and I have sufficient reports that tie him to Amherst Rudd; however, as to his involvement in the death of Jane Chaffin, I have to be honest that it's flimsy at best. I haven't anything that would tie him to a crime while he was here. Still, the timing of his arrival in correlation to her death, cannot be overlooked; especially since, one, there have been no other professional hits reported in the time Dunne was here, except Chaffin's; two, it's simply too coincidental that Dunne, a purported hitman, arrived soon after Chaffin and left shortly after her death; and three, the length of Dunne's stay in Leeds was too short for him to declare it a holiday. It may be flimsy, but I think there's enough there to warrant further investigation."

The superintendent flopped back in his chair and sighed indecisively, "It isn't much, I'll admit, but there is something there; so, tell me what you think you can accomplish in Australia that you can't accomplish using the telephone."

Melissa felt relief flood through her. He hadn't cleared her to go, but he had stopped blatantly shooting down the option of going, "The ME is set to release the type of weapon used in the murder of Jane Chaffin, hopefully soon. Chances are that the murder weapon can be linked to Lachlan Dunne. If we didn't find it here, he may have returned to Australia with it. I can't find that murder weapon on the phone. Moreover, I have a weak link between Dunne and Rudd currently, but if I am in Australia, I may be able to verify that link. Also, I can use the resources at Jane Chaffin's offices to find out why Rudd felt the need to send a hitman across the globe to eliminate her;

---

[3] Omertà – Italian for secrecy sworn to by an oath; a code of silence (DSctionary.com, 2013).

find out what threat she posed to him. Additionally, I can locate and meet with Arran Masters—interview him on his involvement, and work with the local police in getting him into protective custody, if needed. If not all of the police are dirty, I'm going to need their assistance in possibly apprehending Lachlan Dunne, and potentially, Amherst Rudd, in preparation for extradition. I can possibly coordinate some of that over the phone, but for true efficiency and expediency, I need to be there to head up the investigation. If things go the way I hope, I will already be on site to escort Dunne, and possibly Rudd, back to Britain to face a criminal charge of murder—a charge that the Australia police have yet to be able to levy against either man, apparently."

"Flimsy, but I agree that finding the murder weapon and connecting Dunne to Rudd can't be done over the phone—not effectively anyway; and bringing down Amherst Rudd would be a coup, and if he's sending hitmen across the pond, then he needs to be brought to justice. Still, how would Lachlan Dunne get a weapon on board a flight and back? Security measures..."

"Remember the case a few years back of the Arabic assassin that was sent to kill that American Head of State?"

"Vaguely."

"Well, he got around airline security measures by mailing the weapon to himself ahead of time via a private courier to an accomplice. What's to prevent Lachlan Dunne doing the same?"

"So now, we not only have a hitman flying into the country to eliminate people, but we also potentially have someone living here ready, willing, and able to assist in those endeavors. This is sounding more and more like a James Bond novel than an actual case. If not for the dead body, I'd think it was all fantasy." He sighed loudly, nodded thoughtfully, and then speared Melissa with a no-nonsense glare, "If you go, you can't come back empty-handed. It's the only way I can justify the expense. I want Lachlan Dunne in handcuffs, at the very least."

"I understand."

"Come back empty-handed, I will be well within my rights to ship you off to another post. Understand that?"

"I do."

"Willing to take that risk?"

"I am. I think that we have a starting place, and the potential to bring down a mafia boss. I think that we owe it to Jane Chaffin to find her killer, but to also protect the man she herself was trying to protect. Additionally, it wouldn't hurt for us to send a message that we won't allow rabble from other countries to bring their disputes here."

CI Wright rubbed his chin and sighed, as if still debating with himself over whether authorizing his detective sergeant's trip was prudent or foolhardy. Still, this murder case had turned into far more than just the death of a woman. Now there was the potential connection with a mob boss in another country with a worse-than-notorious reputation. If he could see that man brought down, it would be all that was needed to get noticed and possibly take over the coveted chair of Chief Superintendent. A position he'd had his eyes on for years. Before now, he just mentally willed the current chief to choke on a banana and die. Now, this investigation could spearhead his career and help him unseat the current chief. No more envisioning death scenarios. Still, he had one dilemma.

"You mentioned getting assistance from the local police. If reports are right about the corruption, you'll likely have to go it alone; no assist from the local authorities. If a cop is involved, they'll try to tank your investigation, and may even put your life in danger. That means that the only lead you'll have, potentially, is..."

"...any notes Jane Chaffin may have taken related to her own investigation. Thin."

"Transparent. Still think there's something to go after? I admit the thought of bringing down Amherst Rudd's criminal organization has me wanting to send you off on the next flight, but common sense is telling me that you'll not likely be able to. On top of that, sending you down without local support to investigate the man could prove deadly."

"And I still contend that there is enough to warrant it. That woman flew over because she thought there was help to be had. We owe it to her to at least try; and if we happen to topple Amherst Rudd in the process—just call it berries on the tart. An added bonus."

"Let me call Chaffin's employer first. If he's willing to release Chaffin's notes, then we'll call it a go."

"Thank you, sir." Melissa flipped through her notes and read off the number for The Western Australian.

CHAPTER NINE

The following morning, she and a newly invigorated Alastair, boarded Qantas, flight 465, bound for Australia. Jane's former boss, Oliver Carter, the editor-in-chief of The Western Australian newspaper, agreed to release all of Jane Chaffin's notes, so that would be their first stop upon arriving. Their next would be to locate Alastair's brother, Arran—*if* he still lived, or if he was even still in Australia. For Melissa, Arran was a low priority. If they found him, Alastair could warn him, feel justified, and have a happy-go-lucky family reunion—none of which was her concern. Tying Lachlan Dunne to Chaffin's murder took precedence. Even tying Dunne to Amherst Rudd was a secondary priority. It seemed a lot of effort for the death of one woman, but, with any luck, this investigation would start an avalanche that could reveal many more deaths. She only hoped that, once she started the avalanche, she managed to get out of its path in time. The last thing she fancied was dying, and leaving her darling kitty, Kookie, orphaned.

"A shilling for your thoughts." He'd been watching Melissa's face change emotions for the past half hour, so he decided to find out why her brow kept creasing with anger, or concern.

Melissa turned to face Alastair, her gaze taking in his features; her thoughts shifting from Rudd and Dunne to what was driving this man seated beside her. She could better understand his need to warn his brother if his connection to said brother was a strong bond developed since childhood; but Arran was no more than a stranger, so why the obsessive, nearly irrational, need to locate him? Weren't priests supposed to be passive, apathetic individuals who cared only for the souls of their congregation? Yet this priest seemed different somehow. There was a fire in his gaze, a determination in his manner, and assertiveness to his speech; which belied the genteel priestly characters she'd seen portrayed in movies. The only passion those motion picture characters displayed was when they were determined to cast out a demon spirit, or some such nonsense.

"I'll up it from a shilling to a crown if you stop gawking at me like that, and tell me what you're thinking?"

"Oh, sorry." She blinked, but did not reveal any of her thoughts. "You really have been out of society for a long time if you're enticing me with monies no longer in circulation."

Alastair grinned, "I know they aren't currency any longer. It's just something the Father's at the orphanage used to say. Besides, fictional money is all I have to entice with since I depleted my savings for this trip. So, a fictional shilling for your thoughts?"

"My thoughts aren't worth even fictional money, to be honest."

"Very well," he relented and turned the topic to the information he gleaned from Australia House, "According to my research, Arran was fostered out to a Timothy and Barbara Masters, who settled in Fremantle."

"On the west coast. I've never been there, but I do have an aunt that lives in nearby Perth."

"Well, they had a home on Terrace Road, just off the waterfront, not too far from Langley Park."

Melissa didn't miss the past tense in that sentence, "Alastair, please tell me you verified that the Masters *still* live in or around Fremantle, or at the very least verified that they still live on the continent. They could be vital in locating your brother sooner rather than never."

Alastair had the good sense to look chagrinned and Melissa sighed in frustration. She really did want to smack him upside the head. Once she smacked him, she would need to smack her own head for allowing herself to get so distracted as to let a priest commandeer her investigation; an investigation she may have had more control over had she not been busily chasing after this priest, keeping him out of mischief and potential danger. Still, she had to concede, that if not for him, she may not have an investigation to begin with, so she simply sighed. All she could do now was hope that the Masters still resided in Fremantle or left a decent trail to follow if they didn't. Or that Arran Masters wasn't a common name on the continent and they'd be able to track him down before she died of old age. One thing she was certain of—she was going to take a firm control over this investigation. Enough was enough.

CHAPTER TEN

One Month Prior
Perth, Western Australia

"Don't look so disconsolate, Arran," Amherst Rudd cajoled, his tone nauseatingly syrupy. "Consider your discovery fortuitous. Now, I can put you to far better use than just balancing the books; which means that you get a raise in your wages."

Arran sat silent, shivering; gaze downcast and shoulders slumped, his arms wrapped protectively around his midsection. He didn't dare offer a reply—or his much-preferred retort—because he now knew what happened to men that dared counter or cross his boss. His stomach was still roiling over that newfound knowledge.

When Rudd's thug hauled him into the boss's lavish headquarters in downtown Perth, shortly after he gave Jane the boot, Arran thought that he was merely going to hear how he would now be responsible for laundering money for Rudd's illegal venture. That same venture he'd accidentally stumbled across when doing his bi-annual reporting. Illegal laundering had been a bad enough discovery for Arran; a discovery which he wished he could undo; however, the car ride with Rudd's thug had revealed even more about Rudd, which Arran wished he'd not been privy. It was during that ride that Lachlan Dunne regaled Arran with Rudd's numerous secondary enterprises.

Arran felt ill upon discovering the type of man he worked for, but felt downright catatonic when Lachlan offered a demonstration of what happened to those who declined Rudd's offer of advancement, or worse—turned narc.

This demonstration took place immediately upon arrival at Rudd Tower. Instead of going straight to Rudd's offices to speak with his boss, Dunne walked him over to a private elevator, which carried them down into the bowels below Rudd Tower. Level *B4*, according to Dunne. A place he didn't know existed prior to now.

The memory made him want to vomit.

"Sit!" Dunne ordered, shoving Arran onto a hard-backed folding chair. "You'll keep aware, or I'll make certain you do." He didn't need his graduate degree to ascertain the threat. Either he watched that which was about to play out, or he could find himself in similar straights.

Dunne issued an order to another Pit Bull-resembling thug, who disappeared only a few seconds through a closed door on the far side of the room, returning with a bound and gagged bespectacled shrimp of a man. The man may have had duct tape firmly over his mouth, but he was squealing to beat the band. In the far corner of the room was another chair, the same type on which Arran now sat squirming. He didn't know what was about to transpire, but he knew it wasn't going to bode well for the bespectacled shrimp.

Dunne pushed him pitilessly onto the chair, and then bound his legs securely to the chair legs with plastic straps. A second thug worked with zeal, binding the man's torso to the chair with duct tape.

When Dunne was assured the man was secure, he went to a nearby cabinet, reached inside, and pulled out a small glass vial; and then walked over and squatted next to the man. He spoke a language that Arran didn't comprehend, but recognized as Russian, which sounded odd to his ears as it was spoken in Dunne's thick Australian accent. It made him realize that the shrimp must be the Russian. He shook his head in bemusement at his mind's strange wanderings, especially when he realized that the bespectacled shrimp was squealing loudly again.

Dunne's questioning became more insistent, but the shrimp did no more than squeal. Arran's mind drifted again, wondering how any answer was supposed to be supplied if the man's mouth was taped closed. As soon as his mind formulated the thought, Dunne yanked the tape from the man's face, causing him—and Arran—to wince.

Dunne asked the question once more, but it was as if the man's mind had shut down, unable to formulate even a basic sentence or plea. Unintelligible whimpers poured forth, but nothing which Lachlan wished to hear, for he snapped at the man callously, holding the vial just above the man's feet.

The man began to blubber louder, and Lachlan removed the glass dropper from the vial. Arran watched in growing horror, as a large drop of liquid left the dropper and landed with a plop atop the man's bare foot. His whimpering turned *to screams of agony, as that drop quickly ate a half-pence-sized hole through the flesh. Arran's eyes widened and he turned his head to the side and vomited as acidic-smelling burning flesh reached his nostrils.*

Dunne asked the question again, but instead of answering, the man continued to wail. Lachlan drew more acid from the vial and squeezed another drop on the same foot, increasing the size of the hole.

The man passed out.

Dunne gave instructions to the other thug, then left the man's side, hauled Arran up from the chair and pulled his wilted body across the ground to the elevator, dumping him unceremoniously onto the floor inside.

Now Arran sat in Rudd's office, shivering uncontrollably, his arms crossed protectively around his waist. Though he sat directly across from the man whose orders had been responsible for that unfortunate man's suffering, he could not bring himself to look at him.

"Lachlan, get Arran a glass of my Bundaberg Rum," Rudd ordered, watching his CFO carefully. If he didn't get his wits about him, he'd be useless to his business and he'd have to have Lachlan take him below for a bath of the permanent variety. A message he would need to convey to Arran in no uncertain terms. "What you saw down below, was a necessary evil that keeps my businesses running, and my employees loyal. It was because certain dependability came into question today, that a young man had to suffer an irreparable harm. That young man will live—possibly—but his father shall no longer question why I require his services."

"That was a boy?" Arran finally lifted his head and brought his gaze to bear, filled with disbelief, on the well-built man behind his antique kauri desk. "You tortured a boy?"

"Hardly a boy at fourteen. The point I am trying to get across to you, Arran, is that when you work for me, you work for me. There are no whys, no cannots, and no trips to the local police department. Any decrease in efforts or clandestine meetings with persons unknown, will bring your allegiance into question. And if I start to question your allegiance, then I have to discover whether your loyalty is at issue. To do that takes special measures. Any questions?"

"But why the boy? What answers could he have given that would have prevented being tortured?" Arran hadn't heard much of what Rudd said, hadn't gotten past the fact that Rudd was low enough to persecute an innocent child—and for what? To ensure that boy's father continue work unwaveringly? If he hadn't already thrown up his stomach contents, he could easily have done so again—so sick was he at the thought of what Rudd may have done to Jane, had he not broken up with her; had he somehow failed in his duties as Chief Financial Officer for this new undertaking of Rudd's.

"What information? Well, I needed to know whether certain information that had come to my attention was true, about whether his father was speaking to the police; and the boy was in a unique position to know. The father simply denied it—repeatedly. Whether the boy suffers further will be strictly up to whether he decides to tell me about his father's whereabouts of late, and with whom his father met. I could have tortured the father, but if I did, he would be useless to me for some time. This way, I ensure the father's expedient return to his work—if he is innocent as he says; and, by demonstrating my resolve using the boy, I ensure his father's unwavering dedication to that work. Now drink the rum, it will calm your nerves."

Arran reached for the glass and downed the amber liquid in one swig, and then coughed as the fiery fluid burned at the inside of his esophagus. He closed his eyes and felt the glass removed from his hand. The liquid warmth filling his belly did little to quell the fear within his mind; still, it did work to abate the shivers wracking his body, but it would take more than a single glass of rum to forget in whose company he sat. He shook his head, unable to comprehend anything, especially why he was so important as to be brought into the illegal side of his boss' businesses. Did Rudd really fear that he would go to the police with the knowledge he gleaned, and so decide to show him the importance of continued allegiance; decide to entice him with better wages and a lavish lifestyle? He was just a well-educated accountant, so why not just kill him? It's not as if he couldn't be replaced.

"You're probably wondering why I don't just do away with you, aren't you, Arran? It's because I need you. You were always very good about keeping my finances in order, and honest to boot—no skimming off the top, or doctoring the numbers. A rarity among accountants these days, it would seem. So, I want to keep you in the fold. Only now, I want you to work on the business end in the distribution of a new product that my Russian is developing."

"I'm not a businessman or a distributor. I just crunch numbers. I don't know anything about product distribution."

"No worries. You'll continue in your current capacity while I await finalization of my product. When that new product is ready to distribute, you will work hand-in-hand with me in deciding the best, most lucrative, method of circulation. You've done my books long enough to ascertain which segments of society will prove most beneficial—financially—to me."

"I just run the numbers; balance the books. I don't know anything of value." When Rudd just sat staring at him, he decided to affect a brave front, "If I prefer not to enter into this particular part of the business? If I just say no?"

"Think *acid*." Rudd paused for a minute before continuing. "Still want to say no?"

Arran had suddenly become so afraid of the word no, that he couldn't even respond; couldn't even shake his head. He just sat immobile, images of what happened to the young Russian boy flitting through his mind.

"Good. Lachlan will return you to your apartment. You'll go to work tomorrow as usual and Lachlan will come for you when I need you further."

"Business as usual then? I'm not going to work on your *other* books?"

Rudd snorted, "I probably could do with your skills in that area also, but I have a competent man already taking care of that end. You just continue work on my legitimate businesses and ignore any unusual discrepancies or funds movement."

"Why couldn't this other man simply help you when your product is ready? Why do you need me?"

"Why do you think?" Rudd asked, and Arran knew the answer immediately. Get his hands just dirty enough, and he would be unwilling to rat on his boss for fear of taking equal blame in illicit activities. Rudd saw the light of understanding in Arran's eyes and smiled, "I didn't get to where I am by not playing to all of my strengths, and to my rival's—and employees'—weaknesses."

Rudd waved a hand at Lachlan, who clasped hold of Arran's arm, lifting him from the chair. At any other time, he might complain about a big brute manhandling him, but not right now; for if it were not for Lachlan's grip, his legs would not likely hold him. His head hurt, his stomach roiled, and his heart ached. He didn't know how he was supposed to act as if all were fine come tomorrow morning, but for Jane's sake, he had to try. Arran may think her out of the picture; out of harm's way, but that didn't mean that Rudd wouldn't use her against him if he shirked his responsibilities, or gave the slightest hint of being untrustworthy.

****

Jane sat vigil in her car outside of Rudd Tower, trying to put her journalistic talents to work for her, while she waited on Arran to leave. There was definitely more to this than met the eye, and she was going to find out what—for Arran's sake, as well as her own. She refused to believe that he'd dumped her because he'd tired of her. His trivializing of their relationship was a huge tell, but his parting comment about giving regards to someone unknown to her, was even more revealing. He wanted her to know that something was amiss, and now it was up to her to find out what—beginning with what Amherst Rudd's interest was in her man.

She needed to talk to Arran.

She stopped jotting notes when she spotted Arran exit the building. He looked ill and defeated; a look that she'd never seen before and it angered her. She started to get out of the car to go to him, when Rudd's brute exited right behind Arran, clasped his arm, and ushered him to a waiting silver Holden Commodore.

If Rudd's bodyguard was to be playing bodyguard to Arran, then she would have to either find a way to speak to Arran surreptitiously, or determine a different way in which to find answers. Following him around wasn't going to be a very productive manner in which to get results, especially since doing so already revealed the trouble he was in was directly related to Amherst Rudd.

She closed the car door and slipped her Mazda 3 into gear, pulling slowly away from the curb. She turned onto Beaufort Street and headed back to her offices at the Western Australian on Stirling. She was going to need her desktop and her exploratory assistant in order to do some much-needed investigative digging into Amherst Rudd's enterprises—a venture heretofore frowned upon by her editor-in-chief. Well, with or without his approval, she would dig up the information she needed to topple the whole of Rudd Tower, if it meant helping the man she loved.

She pulled into the parking structure and entered her offices a few minutes later with an urgency that the front desk receptionist had grown used to long ago. What the receptionist was unused to was the very-busy journalist stopping by her desk to request a favor.

"Rosemary, isn't it?"

The receptionist nodded, ignoring the buzzing of the phone.

"I know that I don't normally call upon you for assistance, but I would be forever grateful if you could ring up Novick & Associates. Speak to Joshua Nguyen. Have him come by my office in half hour. I have a job for him."

The receptionist nodded, while she quickly jotted down the given instructions.

"I do appreciate the assist. Normally, I would take care of the call myself, but I'm going to be tied up in a meeting for the next half hour and need him here when I'm done."

The receptionist nodded again. Jane smiled and headed for the lifts. It was time to convince her editor that doing an exposé on Rudd was more important than he seemed to think it was. She only hoped he would finally see reason.

CHAPTER ELEVEN

He was being unreasonable!

Once again, he argued that going after Rudd was a pointless endeavor. "It won't result in a news story, unless it happens to be your obituary."

"You're wrong, Oliver, but I can't prove to you that you're wrong unless you give me leave to do so. I'm talking Walkley Award[4] here."

"No, you are talking death sentence."

"And you're talking nonsense. Obviously you know there is more to Rudd's enterprises than meets the eye, or you wouldn't be reluctant—no, downright adamant—about allowing me to investigate what could be the biggest story of my career, the grandest story in this paper's history. What do you know, Oliver? And don't feed me the same old line about simply being leery of writing about one of Australia's powerhouses. There's more to it—to him—and I want to know what that something is. What makes people bow to his will?"

Oliver sat back in his chair and sighed heavily. He'd thus far kept a reign on his top reporter, but there was a new gleam in her eye, which bespoke of more than determination to assuage curiosity over an enigma; it was more a determination to reveal that which he knew shouldn't be revealed. It was an all-too familiar gleam. He sighed again. He'd hoped to prevent a recurrence of history, but he also knew that stopping a reporter with that level of determination, was like trying to prevent a tsunami washing ashore with mere words. It couldn't be done.

"Okay, Jane," he said finally, in soft-spoken resignation, "perhaps there are a few things you should know. Then if you are still determined to dig up some best-left-buried facts—I'll hand you the shovel."

Jane smiled and settled back in her own chair, waiting in eager anticipation. For decades, she'd heard quietly whispered rumors

---

[4] The Walkley Awards for Excellence in Journalism are presented annually in Australia to recognize and reward the best in the craft.

about Amherst Rudd and his bodyguards, but nothing substantiated. When she became a reporter, one of the first curiosities she wanted to alleviate was who this man was, but to no avail. Every question asked was met with silence or rebuke; however, what people refused to accept, was that their reluctance to speak only made her curiouser and curiouser.

"I'll preface my objections to your pursuit with a cautionary tale. One that I hope will make you see reason. A few years before your arrival at my offices, I had in my employ another young promising reporter, whose inquisitiveness rivaled even your own. She was not interested in the mundane, rather sought out those stories that other reporters never even fathomed could be newsworthy. I don't know if you recall some years back that story that nearly brought Tambolane Industries to its knees?"

"From what I remember, that story revealed Tambolane was using substandard materials in the construction of the new levee and warned of the impact on Australians should the Minister for Natural Resources and Mines not heed the warning and stop the levee construction immediately. It was superior investigative work."

"It was indeed, and it was written by Amberly Ibsen."

"Didn't she disappear about seven years ago?"

"She did."

"There's more to this, isn't there?"

Oliver nodded. His lips pursed in exasperated misery as the memory of his star reporter, sitting across from him much as Jane did now, crashed to the forefront, "Just like you, she *knew* with absolute certainty that there was something off about Amherst Rudd; that the persona revealed in public was disingenuous. No evidence mind you, just gut instinct based on rumor and innuendo. A whispered comment over a cocktail or a murmured word from a former employee was all she needed to start digging—and I willingly handed her a shovel. I gave her the permission she wanted, because I, too, was naïve in my beliefs that nothing should be hidden; that no one was above having their true lives revealed for all to read about over a morning cup of cappuccino. My naïveté got her murdered."

"I thought hers was an open case, her disappearance unsolved."

"Unsolved by the police, yes, but far from a mystery to me; and is why I can't make the same mistake with you."

"Oliver, what are you trying to tell me? Do you know what happened to Amberly Ibsen?"

Oliver nodded again, his eyes misting as memories flooded his mind, "A few days after she disappeared, whereabouts unknown even to this day; I had a late-night visitor by the name of Lachlan Dunne."

"One of Rudd's bodyguards?"

Oliver nodded again, "He insinuated that I might consider redirecting my enthusiastic pursuit of knowledge in a different direction and persuade those in my employ to never aim their nosiness in Rudd's direction again."

"A warning."

"A not-so-subtle threat."

"But how do you know that his threat had to do with the disappearance of Amberly? I'm not certain I see a solid connection."

With a massive sigh of resignation, Oliver stood from his chair and made his way over to a painting on the wall. He pulled on the left side revealing the safe behind. With quick, efficient twists of the dial, the lock gave and he tugged on the safe door. He reached to the rear and withdrew a small box, and then returned to his chair. "I must trust that what I am going to divulge to you will remain in strictest confidence. I know you are a reporter, but you are also a friend, and as such can you keep my secret? If not, then I will return this box to the safe and burn it just prior to my death."

"I'll keep quiet."

"Why I don't burn it now, I can only surmise that it serves as a painful reminder," he murmured and then fell silent, gazing at the box with anguish glazing his vision. Slowly, he slid the box across his desk and closed his eyes against the onslaught of memories. Jane reached down to pick it up, her brow knitted in confusion and concern. She'd known Oliver for nearly ten years—first as a friend and then as a boss—and never had she seen anything get to him the way the contents of this one small package appeared to be doing now. His reaction made her leery, and reluctant to find out what the contents were; however, the reporter in her overruled any concerns and she slowly lifted the lid revealing within a lady's garnet ring nestled atop a small piece of paper. Her brow knitted again, as she lifted the ring and pulled out the paper. One word was scrawled in what appeared to be crimson ink—*Remember.*

She looked back at Oliver, who sat staring at her with tears streaming down his face. He drew in a shuddered breath and sniffled loudly before answering her unspoken question, "That was Amberly's ring," he whispered shakily, "and it is her blood that was used to write that word. Do you still want that shovel?'"

CHAPTER TWELVE

Jane sat deep in thought, pondering over Oliver's question. Did she want that shovel? His permission to delve into Rudd's affairs? If he gave that permission, would he end up receiving a small box with one of her possessions and a single word written in her blood? Doubt warred with love. Love won.

"Arran is in trouble. Somehow, he's gotten mixed up in Rudd's world. If I'm going to help him, I need to find out what it is about Rudd that makes people so damned afraid of him. I now know that Arran dumped me this morning in an effort to keep me safe. If he can do that to protect me, I should be willing to do the same for him."

"I'm sorry to hear about Arran," Oliver said softly, then retrieved a tissue from the box on his desk and blew his nose loudly. "He's a good man if he's willing to do that for you, but getting yourself killed isn't necessarily going to ensure his safety, is it? On top of that, if Arran dumped you to protect you, as you say, then it's likely because Rudd knows who you are, and that you're a reporter. Start sticking your nose into his business, and he's going to know your motives for doing so. Did you miss the part of my story about how Amberly's whereabouts are still unknown, even to this day? Do you think her disappearance coincidental to her digging into Rudd's Enterprises? Did you forget the warning I just showed you? Do you really love Arran so much that you're willing the risk the same fate? Not to mention, you could be putting his life in danger even more than it is potentially already. On top of that, I don't happen to want another late night visit from one of Rudd's thugs bearing another memento."

Jane sat quietly for a few moments, as if absorbing everything her editor was telling her. Yes, she was afraid, especially now that she knew what kind of man Rudd truly was. No longer was his reputation rumored, but factual, back up by someone for whom she had the greatest respect. That scared her, but what scared her more was Arran's obvious unwilling involvement with Rudd. Whatever hold

Rudd had on Arran, it was enough to make him worry for her safety; enough to make him break it off with her in an effort to protect her. If he cared that much for her, should she not be willing to risk her own self for him? And then there was his parting comment to her. "Arran mentioned a man by the name of Alastair this morning. Perhaps Arran thought this person is able to provide the help needed. If he's a stranger, Rudd would have no reason to suspect him of anything." She didn't mention that Arran thought this man was his brother.

"Just you contacting this man could raise flags in Rudd's offices. You could unwittingly be putting someone else's life in danger. Jane, I know I said that I'd hand you that shovel if you insisted on digging around for information on Rudd, but I can't do so in good conscience. I can't be the one responsible for your death, so if you decide to go after Rudd, it will be without my blessing or the backing of this newspaper. Do you understand?"

Jane nodded. "I understand, and I sincerely appreciate the position you're in; but I want you to try to understand that I cannot leave the man I love to fend for himself against a man like Amherst Rudd. Somehow, someway, I have to help him."

"I am trying to understand, but the most I can do in support is to wish you success."

"If there's a story in this..."

"There won't be."

Jane nodded again and sighed, and then stood and made her way out of her editor's office. When the door closed behind her, Oliver slid a notepad and pen from the top of his desk and began writing out two things—an ad for a new lead reporter, and Jane's obituary.

CHAPTER THIRTEEN

When Jane neared her desk, the investigator she'd sent for was waiting for her. Joshua Nguyen was the only investigator she ever requested work with her because he was the only man she trusted to get the job done—quickly, accurately, and unfailingly. Never once had his information come into question and never once had he tried to pass off information as being from "an anonymous source". He always provided viable, verifiable leads and reliable data. She trusted him; however, now she worried that by employing him again, she could be putting his life at risk...she shook her head—everyone involved with Rudd and in her investigation had the potential for dying; and if she weren't a bulldog reporter, she would toss her determination to find answers into her mental trashcan and send Justin away. Unfortunately for him, she'd never been able to let go of something once resolve sprouted. She pasted on a smile and extended her hand.

"Hello Joshua," she greeted enthusiastically, pumping his hand exaggeratedly. "Thank you for coming on such short notice. I have a person I need found."

Joshua quirked a brow, but chalked up her uncharacteristic behavior as excitement over a potential story, "Jane, good to see you again. What is it you need me to dig into?"

"Not so much digging this time; rather researching." She knew that he could view this type of assignment as demeaning to his talents, but after her conversation with Oliver, she couldn't risk his life by having him investigate Rudd; however, if she sent him to locate Alastair, Rudd would have no reason to be suspicious.

"Researching is your job, not mine. Mine's investigating."

"I know, but this is important." She reached for a pen and tablet and jotted down *Alastair (surname unknown)*, and then ripped the page from the tablet and passed it to Joshua. "I cannot express deeply enough the importance of finding this man."

"Do you have any notion how popular the name..."

"I'm not leaving you completely clueless, Joshua. I know that he's related, somehow, to my fiancé, Arran Masters. That's A-R-R-A-N," she spelled, as he started jotting notes. "I do not believe, however, that they bear the same surname. If there is any information at all to be found about this man, it may very well come from Arran's parents."

"If this is Arran's brother..."

"Arran was adopted. He didn't even know about a brother until a month past."

"I like you, Jane, but isn't this something you could do yourself? Just run over to Arran's parents and ask a few questions. Why do you need me for such a simple task? It seems a waste of your money and my time and talent."

"I know it does," Jane conceded, and then placed her most charming smile on her face. "Still, I have been called out on a different lead and can't follow up both simultaneously. You're the only investigator I trust. I know if I hire you, I can rely on you to find what I need in a timely manner. I also know that your data will be accurate."

Joshua sighed, "I'm not certain I like you playing me, Jane. I know how good I am without you stroking my ego."

"Then how about I pad your expense account with a few extra dollars to help soothe the irritation on utilizing your skills on such a mundane assignment?"

Joshua's mouth tightened, but no matter his irritation, he wouldn't pass up the offer of extra money, "Can I know why this man is so important? Maybe then I won't feel as if I'm being sent on a fool's errand."

Jane thought about it a moment, deciding how much to reveal. How much did she really know that she could reveal? All she had to go on was her fiancé's parting comment about giving regards to Alastair. Was that just his way of clueing her into the fact that something was wrong; or did Alastair have information that could disentangle her fiancé from the troubles he was in and Arran needed her to know that? Whatever Arran's reasoning, he wanted her to know of Alastair's existence; and she would not be a good reporter or a loving fiancé, if she didn't follow up on that lead.

She really did like Joshua and didn't want to place him in danger. At the same time, however, she needed him to give his best or he might be less willing to do so if he felt this assignment unworthy of his skill. She decided to choose her words carefully.

"Arran is in trouble. He's gotten himself mixed up in shady dealings with nefarious men—and I can't say who...yet. His brother may be his only hope of helping him—if we can find him in time. At least Arran seems to think he may be able to help. I won't know until I find him and question him."

"Who's his brother? Superman?" Joshua quipped, not buying her explanation at all.

"I'm serious, Joshua," Jane said softly, and the smile left Joshua's face. "I'm very concerned that Arran could die. I tried to help him, but he shut me out. If we find his brother, then perhaps he can help get Arran out of this mess; and together, perhaps, we can bring an end to some seriously corrupt persons."

Joshua eyed the journalist for a few moments, and then nodded slightly. "Parents' names?"

"I don't know," Jane admitted, her cheeks tinting red.

"He's your fiancé, but you don't even know his parents' names? Really, Jane? How long have you known this man—a week? No wonder you couldn't just pop 'round and talk to them yourself," he muttered, jotting *parents unknown* on his notepad.

"He just always referred to them as his parents—not by name."

"Well, since his last name is Masters, that's a good place to start. I'll check adoption records and see what I turn up. Do you happen to know his birthday or adoption date; in which city his parents reside: anything that will assist me in not spending the next decade digging through dusty files?"

"He was adopted out through the British £10 POM Program, if that helps."

Joshua nodded, making a notation in his notepad, "It does, yes. That will narrow the search field considerably. In fact, I may have the information you need before the end of business day today."

"That's wonderful, but remember, I need you to find the brother, not just locate Arran's parents."

"Oh yeah, right," Joshua said, scribbling something else in his notepad. "Find brother," he murmured to himself. "Okay, I'll have information this evening, but finding the brother may take a bit longer."

"I figured it might."

"Okay, smartass, I get why you needed me."

Jane laughed, "This search is definitely more than I have time for, but it really is urgent."

Joshua nodded and stood, "I'll do my best."

"I know you will," Jane stood and followed Joshua to the elevators, "and thank you."

Joshua clasped her out-stretched hand, "I still expect a decent bonus."

Jane laughed, "I'll see to it."

CHAPTER FOURTEEN

Present Day
Perth, Western Australia

The moment the plane touched down on the tarmac, Melissa pulled out her phone and rented a car; to be ready at the terminal upon debarkation. As soon as she disconnected that call, she pulled out her iPad, connected with the flight's WiFi, and then pulled up a listing of available hotels in the area. She found one that was within her budgetary restrictions, but then stopped shy of placing the reservation. She turned to Alastair, "What's your budget like for a room rental?"

"About a hundred pounds a night should ensure I'm not left penniless."

Melissa returned her attention to the screen and quickly converted pounds to the Australia dollar—about 2.14AUD to 1GBP[5]. The rooms she was looking at ranged from 150AUD to 250AUD.

"Okay, I think I found suitable lodgings," she started and then paused again. Initially she was going to suggest they get separate rooms, but knew that if she were on a tight stipend, then a priest would have even less available funds for additional expenditures. "I can book us a room with double beds. It would save us both considerable funds if we split costs—unless your religion forbids you rooming with a police woman."

"Not at all," Alastair said, but the red tint creeping up beneath his collar belied his calm words. "Um, I'll just give you the money..."

"Just hold on to it. The room is going to run 250AUD. I'll just let you buy our meals until we're square. Okay?"

Alastair nodded, and Melissa quickly punched in the information to complete their reservation. She'd no sooner closed her laptop when she was back on her phone.

"You're a busy beaver."

---

[5] This was the conversion rate at the time this book was written. Exchange rates vary continually, so may vary from what is written here.

Melissa smiled, but her reply was interrupted when her call connected.

Western Australian. How may I direct your call?

"This is Detective Sergeant Melissa Lloyd, of the Leeds Police. Your Editor-in-Chief, Oliver Carter, is expecting my call."

One moment please.

A second later a man answered, *DS Lloyd. Has your flight arrived?*

The sadness in the man's voice startled Melissa, but she couldn't afford to play psychologist right now, not with a crime to solve. She needed to remain in police mode, "We're taxiing to the terminal as we speak. I'd like to head over to your office as soon as I've picked up my rental car."

She heard a sigh over the receiver and then silence.

"Mr. Carter? Are you still there?"

Yes, sorry. Of course. I have everything that Jane was working on prior to...prior...

"Very good," Melissa interjected, sensing the man was nearing an emotional breakdown. "I won't keep you long then; unless you're able to think of anything I'll need to be informed of, outside of what is in the files."

No, no. Nothing. Just...I just have...it isn't much, I'm afraid. Um, her investigation...it, um...well, it...

"Why don't we just speak when I arrive? Our plane has reached the terminal and we are about to disembark."

Very good.

The call disconnected rapidly and Melissa drew in a deep breath.

"We're not going to Fremantle first?" Alastair asked, trying to keep the irritation from his tone; not that Melissa paid attention.

"Can you drive?"

"Um, yes, of course."

"Okay, if you'll allow me to stop by the murder victim's offices first to retrieve her files, you can drive us to Fremantle, while I read through them. Is that a fair compromise, considering that this trip is meant to catch murderers first, and locate your brother second?"

Alastair had the sense to look chagrined, "I apologize; however, if my brother is still alive, he is mixed up in this somehow, which means his own life could be in danger. I know that a woman is dead, Melissa, but I'd rather my brother not be next."

CHAPTER FIFTEEN

It took two wrong turns, despite the GPS installed in the car, and an hour weaving through traffic to arrive at The Western Australian newspaper offices.

"We should have made that drive in twenty minutes. Next time we need to plan our arrival so that we're not trying to make our way around during rush hour," She yanked open the front door of the building and stormed up to the front desk receptionist. She took a few deep breaths while crossing the short expanse, because she didn't want to take her agitation out on those from whom she needed assistance.

"I'm Detective Sergeant Lloyd of the Leeds Police Department," she stated, revealing her badge. "We're here to see Oliver Carter."

"Of course. Third floor. I'll let him know you've arrived," she replied politely and then directed a delivery man in the same manner.

When the elevator reached the third floor, the delivery man peeled off and reached the third floor receptionist before Melissa and Alastair departed the elevator.

"In a bit of a rush, isn't he?" Alastair whispered.

"As big and brawny as he is, I'm surprised he can move so fast."

"If he looked up from the floor occasionally, he might be less prone to collide with people," Alastair whispered as they moved to stand behind the man; who awaited the receptionist's signature with an impatient tap of his foot. He pushed past Melissa as he turned to leave, and she wanted to pull out her badge and arrest him for being a jackass; however, since she was on foreign soil, she had to relinquish the urge.

"Detective Lloyd, if you will follow me, Mr. Carter is expecting you. Can I get you or your companion a cup of tea?" The receptionist asked, retrieving the package and heading toward the editor's office.

"I'm fine, thank you. Alastair?"

"I'm fine also."

She knocked on the editor's office and then entered, "You have a package, Mr. Carter, and your appointment has arrived."

"Thank you, Connie," he acknowledged, and then waved his guests to chairs in front of his desk. He immediately set the box to the side and then placed a flash drive in front of Melissa. "This is every file related to Amherst Rudd that I found on Jane's computer. It isn't much. She'd only just begun to dig before...well...before...anyway, um, I know this is cliché, but if anyone requests to know where you obtained this information..."

"We'll leave your name out of it."

Oliver nodded, "People who stick their noses in Rudd's business don't often fair well."

"They end up dead," Melissa concluded bluntly. "Like Jane."

Oliver nodded, "She isn't the only one of my reporters to have suffered death's fate for poking around where they oughtn't. I've lost two brilliant reporters..." He shook his head and drew in deep breaths, his lips pursing in anger as he tried to get control of his emotions.

"We're sorry for your losses, Mr. Carter," Alastair said softly. "I know it's small consolation, but your assistance may very well prevent the death of more people."

"We hope," Melissa clarified quickly, not wanting to provide false hope that they'd be able to do what no other local law enforcement had been able to do to date—bring down Amherst Rudd.

"Or it could bring about more deaths," Oliver replied morosely.

"Do you happen to know an acquaintance of Jane's by the name of Arran Masters?" Melissa interjected quickly, certain that this man's pending emotional breakdown was closer than anticipated earlier.

"Arran, yes. I've never met him, but Jane mentioned that she was after Rudd because of Arran. They were involved, you see. Arran and Jane. She said that Arran had somehow gotten mixed up in Rudd's business. She was determined to find out how and to get him uninvolved. Instead, she ended up dead. I warned her it could happen, but she was stubborn...brilliantly stubborn. I knew it would happen. I even wrote out her obituary the day she requested permission to investigate Rudd. Maybe my presumption sealed her fate, I don't know."

"Mr. Carter," Melissa interrupted his gloomy self-lashing. "I know how distressing this is for you, but is there anything more that you can tell us, which will assist in our investigation? Anything not in the file?"

The prompt brought to mind the garnet ring in the box at the back of his safe, but he wouldn't mention that. It wasn't pertinent anyway, as far he was concerned. He shook his head, "I can't think of anything else that could help. What's in those files is everything she had an opportunity to work on during the short time she was investigating."

"Um, Mr. Carter, you said that she and Arran were involved. Did they happen to reside together?" Arran asked softly, also mindful of the man's deteriorating state.

"She didn't mention living with Arran. I don't think she did."

"She wouldn't happen to have mentioned where Arran lived, by chance?"

Oliver shook his head and Alastair sighed.

Melissa stood and stretched her hand out. Oliver clasped it and then escorted them from the office.

"I'll leave my card for you. If you think of anything pertinent, please ring me up on my mobile number."

"I will." Oliver slipped that card into his vest pocket and then returned to his desk. Abstractly, he reached for the package that arrived. He slid the letter opener through the tape, his mind still on the detective sergeant's visit. Was there anything further he could do to aid in the investigation, without endangering his own life? He genuinely couldn't think of anything. He sighed and pulled the box flaps open.

Inside the small box lay another smaller box. His eyes widened and his heart began palpitating. It was identical to the box in his safe. This time, however, it had not been hand-delivered with a menacing threat; a delivery man had brought it in; just like regular post. Perhaps he was just making more of the similarities than there were. Gingerly he reached inside and withdrew the box. Perspiration broke out all over his face, and his breathing grew shallow as he slowly lifted the lid.

He closed his eyes and tears began to pour down his cheek. Jane's special journalist pendants—a pewter newspaper beside a tiny bronze camera—lay nestled atop a folded piece of paper. His breathing was jagged as he lifted the gold chain and lay the pendant aside. He didn't want to view the note; but he had to know.

He swallowed hard and then opened the parchment.

You were warned was scrawled in crimson, and he knew the killer had written it in Jane's blood.

CHAPTER SIXTEEN

"How long to Fremantle?" Melissa asked, pulling her laptop from its case and settling it on her lap.

"According to the GPS, we should be there in about half hour," Alastair replied, pulling onto State Route 2.

Melissa stuck the flash drive into her USB port and opened the file folders, giving them a cursory inspection. "Do try to ensure that we arrive in one piece, please?" She quipped, as Alastair swerved to avoid a car that cut precariously close to their bumper during a hasty lane change.

"Tell that to that man!" Alastair snapped, his hands gripping tightly to the wheel.

Melissa grinned, "Been a while since you've driven?"

"A while," Alastair admittedly sheepishly.

"Then I'll reiterate, try not to get us killed," she stated, more seriously, then returned her attention to her laptop, clicking on a subfolder titled 'Gambling', and then read the information that Jane had typed into a Word document: *Two hotels, front for illegal gambling operations. Yacht in Rudd's name—front for gambling? Funds funneled where?* Melissa stopped scanning. *Hardly hard evidence*, she thought. *Circumstantial at best.*

The notes proved more thoughts than evidence, stating that, if gambling were one of Rudd's enterprises, he'd most likely utilize banks in Costa Rica to funnel funds. The notes ended—*More investigation needed.*

She clicked on three more subfolders: Prostitution, Extortion, Sex Trafficking. All of which contained similar notes to investigate further.

"Nothing here, thus far," Melissa said frustrated, and then clicked on a folder labeled 'Legitimate businesses'. There were three subfolders: 'Harness the Sun Solar Companies', 'ABL Bowling Centers' and 'Della Polpetta Restaurants'. She clicked on the Word Document in one and, although the information was as scant and useless as in the illegal activities folders, this one did hold a snippet that could be useful—that Arran was Rudd's accountant for the legitimate industries in which Rudd was co- or full-owner.

"Your brother's an accountant for Amherst Rudd." Melissa stated matter-of-factly, closing the laptop and pulling the flash drive.

"Think he's crooked and Rudd caught on?"

Melissa shook her head, "I don't really know much of anything, and won't until we locate and question your brother. It wouldn't do either of us any good to over-speculate."

"Oliver Carter said that people who stick their noses into Amherst Rudd's business tend to get it lopped off. Are we sure we want to risk our lives and Arran's life by getting too involved?"

Melissa's gaze narrowed and she tried to ferret out Alastair's motivations, "Precisely how do you propose that we solve the murder of your brother's girlfriend, if we don't stick our noses in, hmm? Or did you think that this was just going to be some joyous family reunion where we all pretend everything is hunky-dory?"

"You don't need to get snippy, Melissa. I just think we should consider how we're going to approach this. If we go in, guns blazing, we may as well write our own obituaries right now. I'm proposing, since we are in search of my brother, that we use that to our advantage."

Melissa pursed her lips thoughtfully for a moment, "I'm sorry. I'm a cop, so I tend to latch onto the evidence that will lead me to the killer. Thinking outside of that particular box is not easy; so, I'll hear what you have to say. What do you have in mind?"

"That we approach this just like you said—as a happy reunion. That way if Rudd, or his thugs, get suspicious, they won't find anything that will cause them to get antsy and start shooting."

Melissa nodded thoughtfully, "Okay that actually sounds logical."

Alastair laughed, "Just because I'm a priest doesn't make me a dolt. I am capable of rational thought."

"You know, that's the first time I've heard you laugh," Melissa said impulsively, admiringly.

Alastair turned and looked at her briefly, a wistful smile on his face, "I used to smile frequently, and laugh even more."

"And then a woman died in your confessional," Melissa replied, assumingly.

Alastair shook his head, "That didn't help, but no. I stopped smiling a while ago."

"I thought priests were supposed to be happy go-lucky men who only frowned when a parishioner broke a cardinal rule, or some such."

"Not around priests much, are you?"

"I'm not Catholic."

"Ah, well, most priests of my acquaintance are rather taciturn, but I never believed that collar and crabby should go hand-in-hand, so I endeavor...endeavored...to smile as often as was feasible."

"What happened to change that?"

Alastair spotted the exit for Fremantle then pulled into a nearby petrol station. He turned off the motor and then turned slightly in his seat so that he could face Melissa more directly, "I started to question my faith. There were doubts that surfaced one morning over my cornflakes. I don't know why they came on as they did, but suddenly I doubted my very existence. Why was I Catholic, why was I a priest? I no longer felt priestly. It was as if God was testing me; or, it could have been Satan implanting doubts, slowly killing my faith."

"That why you snapped at me when I called you Father? Has your faith died then?"

"Not my faith in God, no; Catholicism, yes. I don't believe I'll be donning the collar again in this lifetime."

"I'd say that I'm sorry to hear that, but I can tell you aren't meant to be a priest."

Alastair grinned, "And how did you reach that conclusion?"

Melissa shrugged, "I don't know. Just a feeling. I've not met any priests before, but something in my gut tells me that you are atypical of what a priest is supposed to represent."

Alastair nodded, "You'd be right there. So, now that we've reached Fremantle, Detective Sergeant, how do we find the Masters?"

Melissa sighed, "I probably could have done this already, but though I am a great multi-tasker, I have to prioritize those tasks. Okay, let's see here." She picked up her laptop and punched in "White pages Fremantle Australia" into her search engine. After a few more key strokes, she grinned, "Well, well. We got lucky. They still live here. Punch 84 B Forrest Street into the GPS," she instructed.

"We're not going into the police department first?"

Melissa shook her head, "I don't recall saying we were going to elicit the assistance of the local police. Besides, even if I did trust the police to help us out, it wouldn't be the Freemantle police; it would be the police in Perth."

"Oh, but you did mention calling them; and I just assumed that we'd be involving them."

"We can't. Rumor has it that a majority of the police are on Rudd's payroll. That slipped my mind when I initially mentioned involving them."

"What you mean to say is we're on a trapeze without a safety net. No backup guns to aid in our protection?" Melissa nodded and Alastair closed his eyes, shaking his head in disbelief, "I just assumed that we'd have help."

"Then you assumed wrong. If you don't think you want to continue, I'll drive you to airport and then go and locate Arran's parents on my own. It was your idea to come to your brother's rescue though, remember?"

Alastair laid his head on the steering wheel, drawing in deep, calming breaths. It took another minute before he was calm enough to look at Melissa again.

"Look, we've got a solid here, so let's follow it up; see where it leads. If anyone can help us find Arran, it'll be his parents, right? It's early enough that we shouldn't be intruding on any meal time. If they're retired, we may catch them at home."

"Let's just hope they didn't depart on a month-long Greek holiday," Alastair quipped, pulling out of the parking lot.

"Something you'd like to do, no doubt?" Melissa asked, noting the wistful tone in which he remarked the comment.

"Australia was all this priest could afford for the moment. I guess I'll have to find an actual job when I get back to Leeds. Start earning an income. Not going to be easy for a man nearing retirement age."

"Retirement age? You couldn't be more than fifty. People nowadays don't seek retirement until seventy-two at the earliest. You've plenty of time to enter the ho-hum existence of the everyday individual."

"Wow, that didn't sound pessimistic or cynical at all," Alistair quipped and Melissa let out a heavy sigh.

"Life just isn't strawberries and wine or fairytales. It's hard work, day in and day out. It's surviving best possible until retirement and then hoping you stashed away enough not to rely on governmental support in your old age. Sad, but it's a fact. You may not realize it, but you've got a good thing going being a priest. No worries over things like rent and bills..."

"You really aren't familiar with priests at all," Alastair interrupted, but before he could enlighten her, the GPS droned for them to make a right and that their destination would be on their left. Once more, the GPS was wrong.

"Unless they live in the middle of the commercial district in the back of a pet store, I'd say we need to be more precise in what we input into the GPS," Alastair laughed, but Melissa was anything but amused.

"It's a piece of junk," she snapped, pulling her laptop and re-checking the address given by Google Maps. "Did you input 84 B Forrest Street?"

"I believe so. Is that F-O-R-E-S-T?"

"Two Rs," Melissa confirmed.

"Ah, I see my mistake. I forgot the "B" and spelled Forrest with one R. Let me correct it, and we should be good to go."

Ten minutes later, they pulled into a large residential area near Frank Gibson Park. They slowed their speed, searching for the house number for the Master's home.

"There!" Alastair called, pulling in front of a red-bricked dwelling.

"There's a car in the drive, so we may be in luck. Okay, let's go find out where your brother lives."

Alastair nodded, drawing in a relieved breath, before shutting off the car engine.

Melissa rang the bell and they waited for a response; her more patiently than Alastair, who stood tapping his foot and twisting his hands.

"You okay? It's not as if these are your parents, whom you're meeting for the first time."

"I know, but they are my brother's parents."

Melissa grinned and shook her head, "Yeah that would make me nervous too."

Alastair didn't miss the sarcasm in her tone, but before he could respond, the door opened and an elderly woman greeted them, with far more enthusiasm than either anticipated.

"Oh my good Lord above! We weren't expecting you today," she exclaimed, pulling open the screen door and launching herself into Alastair's embrace. "Well, for goodness sake, get inside," she continued, bustling the two into the small living room. "You must be Jane. It is so good to meet you finally, my dear. Arran goes on and on about you, but has never deemed it necessary to bring you 'round to meet us. Hold on, Dearie, I'll run get your father. Sit down, sit down!"

Alastair and Melissa stood rooted, staring after the whirlwind, uncertain as to what transpired.

"What just happened?" Melissa asked softly.

"Um, I don't know," Alastair responded, equally quiet.

Melissa's gaze moved around the living space and then her eyes widened in surprise. "Alastair, I think you need to look at this," Melissa said, moving toward the fireplace. She picked up a photo from the mantle, looked it over, and then handed it to Alastair.

Before he could register what he was looking at, the Masters returned.

"Hello, son, it's good to see you, but you know you should have called," the elderly man boomed. Alastair turned and the man took a step back, "You aren't Arran," he accused, suspicion lacing his tone.

"Did you forget to take your meds again this morning, Sweetheart," his wife cooed, "Of course it's Arran."

Timothy Masters shook his head, "No, it's not. Arran has green eyes. This man has blue eyes."

Melissa instinctively turned to look at Alastair's eyes, but Alastair was looking down at his spitting image in the photo. Try as he might, he couldn't discern the eye color of the man looking back at him.

"Who are you and what are you doing in our home, impersonating our son?" Neither Melissa nor Alastair responded quickly enough for Timothy, so he reached inside a nearby closet and retrieved a rifle, which he cocked and aimed in their direction.

Barbara Masters was finding it all a bit too much to absorb and started crying, "What are you doing, Timothy? Have you lost your mind?"

"Look at his eyes, woman! Don't you know the color of your own son's eyes?"

Melissa chose that moment to reach into her pocket to retrieve her badge. This was getting out of hand fast, and getting them nowhere even faster.

"Sir, I'm Detective Sergeant Melissa Lloyd of the Leeds Police Department; and this is Alastair Fildew, former priest at St. Gregory's Church, also in Leeds. We're here to talk to you about your son, Arran."

"So, you aren't Jane then? Is Arran alright?" Barbara exclaimed. "If you are from Leeds, why do you look exactly like my son?"

"Except for the eyes," Timothy muttered, lowering his rifle.

"I...um," Alastair started, but was still having difficulty locating his voice.

"We're here because of Arran and Jane. Perhaps we could all take a seat?" Melissa asked and started toward the couch. When she noticed Alastair wasn't moving, she backtracked, took his hand, and led him to the couch. "Sit," she instructed. "Mr. and Mrs. Masters, you may wish to take a seat also," she prodded when they didn't move either.

When everyone had taken a seat, Melissa launched into the reason for the visit, "You mentioned Jane, Mrs. Masters. I know you said you've never met her, but I still need to inform you that Jane Chaffin died in Leeds a few days ago. We're here investigating her murder, which is why we need to locate and speak with your son, Arran."

"Surely you don't think our son..." Timothy started, but Melissa interrupted him.

"Certainly not, Mr. Masters, and I'm truly sorry if it sounded as if I implied that. No, we think that whoever killed Jane may also intend harm toward Arran. We need to locate him, but have no idea as to his current whereabouts."

"Why do you look so much like my son?" Barbara whispered, her gaze scanning Alastair intently.

Melissa sighed, realizing that their visit had sent the elder woman, already emotionally charged over her "son's" visit, into a near state of shock, which made it impossible for her to comprehend anything other than the man seated in her living room bearing a striking resemblance to her boy.

Alastair looked at Melissa seeking confirmation that it would be okay to veer from the purpose of their visit long enough to set an elderly woman's mind to rest. Melissa nodded at him, giving him the permission he sought.

"I've only recently been made aware that I may be Arran's brother."

"Arran had a brother?" Timothy asked, incredulous.

Alastair nodded, "Apparently Arran was adopted out through the £10 POM Program, but they decided not to adopt us out together...well, not to adopt me out at all. I spent my youth in a boy's home."

"Dear Lord! Well, know this, son," Timothy said, his voice full of emotion and conviction, "that had we known Arran had a brother that needed a home, we would have gladly taken you in as well."

"We simply hadn't known," Barbara added, tears glistening in her eyes. "Oh, dear boy, you never had a mother or father?"

Alastair shook his head and pursed his lips, struggling to keep his own tears at bay. He nodded to the elderly couple and sniffed loudly, "I appreciate your kindness."

"So, then, you've done okay with yourself?" Barbara asked, swiping at her nose again. "Become an Inspector?"

Alastair shook his head, "No, a priest." He ignored the fact that Melissa had stated that earlier; however, he understood the shock this elderly woman was in over his appearance.

"You were raised Catholic?" Timothy asked, eyes wide.

Alastair nodded, wondering why the surprise. Surely these people hadn't known his parents; wouldn't know of any religious affiliation he might have had prior to becoming a priest. Not that it mattered, since he wasn't a priest any longer—or Catholic.

"Well, that's just fine also," Barbara muttered, simultaneously swiping a tissue across her nose, and jabbing her husband lightly on the arm. "I do apologize for interrupting the reason for your visit," she said to Melissa, her tone stiff. "I just had to know. You understand? Now why would my son be in danger? You do know that his fiancé is...was...a reporter, and reporters are known for getting themselves into situations from which it would be rather hard to extract themselves?"

"My wife is correct; and while we're sorry to hear about her demise, I'm not certain that it would have had anything to do with our son."

"Perhaps you'd better explain, since you were the one with direct contact with Jane prior to her death," Melissa said to Alastair whose eyes widened slightly at the request. He wasn't certain he wanted to relive the incident at the church; yet at the same time, Melissa was right, no one knew better the circumstances that led them here today. He nodded solemnly, then turned back to address the Masters.

"Jane came to visit me at the church. She specifically said that Arran was in danger and thought that, perhaps, I was in a position to help him." He stopped, shaking his head in remembrance. "Until she arrived, I hadn't even been aware that I had a brother; and, to this day, I'm not certain of what I can do if Arran does turn out to be mixed up in something dangerous. That's why Melissa is here with me. She's the police officer; the one with the skills to assist if Arran does turn out to need help. Me? I was just a priest that a young lady felt the need warn; someone she thought might could help her fiancé; and since Arran is my brother, the least I can do is my best."

"We don't know what kind of trouble Arran could be into. He certainly never mentioned anything to us. He's just an accountant— an innocuous job, if there ever was one," Timothy answered, sighing heavily. "Still, if Jane came to you for help—all the way in England— then she must have known something that we didn't know; but I must confess to being a little confused by her decision. What help could a priest give?" Before anyone could offer an answer to his apparently rhetorical query, he rose, "I'll get his address for you." Timothy left the room, leaving them sitting in uncomfortable silence with Barbara, who sat staring awkwardly at Alastair. Apparently, despite all she'd been told, she was having difficulty wrapping her mind around the fact that her son had a twin brother.

"Why would Jane think a priest—in England, no less—would be able to help Arran if he were in danger?" She asked, reiterating her husband's question, her brow knitting in deep confusion, which made

Melissa and Alastair's brow knit also. During this entire time, neither had asked themselves that question, yet it was a very valid question.

"I hadn't gotten around to thinking on that," Alastair replied softly. "I simply couldn't get past knowing that I had a brother out there with whom I was unacquainted. Perhaps Jane thought that the church might have the power to intervene..." Alastair stopped speaking, uncertain how to address that particular question; a question for which he truly had no answer, and from the look on Melissa's face, she couldn't think of a justifiable reason for Jane to fly halfway 'round the world to find Alastair either.

"Perhaps when we find Arran, he'll be able to shed some light on all of this." Melissa offered.

Just then, Timothy returned with an address book, flipping pages as he settled onto the sofa next to his wife, "Arran's address—last we know of anyway—is Adelaide Terrace, East Perth WA 6004. We don't have a flat number though; never really needed it, I guess, since he always visited us; never other way 'round. You'll have to inquire after that when you get there. Just a quick question before you go?"

"Certainly," Melissa confirmed, closing her notepad.

"I know I asked before, but do you *know* why Jane would think a priest could help our son?"

Melissa, Alastair, and Barbara all glanced at each other with an ironic smirk, "That's what they're hoping to find out, my dear," Barbara whispered, patting her husband on the hand.

"Ah, well, I do hope that Arran isn't in any trouble, and I do hope that you find whoever was responsible for Jane's death. I...we...never met the young lady, but if Arran cared for her, then she must have been a good girl; and she certainly didn't deserve to die so young."

Nor in such a brutal fashion, Alastair thought, standing to leave.

The Masters stood also and led them to the front door.

"If you need anything further, you know where to find us, and do have Arran phone as soon as he's able, to let us know he's all right?" Barbara offered.

"We will and we certainly appreciate your offer to help," Melissa said, shaking each of their hands.

"If you, uh, ever want to...well, you know..." Timothy started, clearing his throat.

Alastair smiled, "I'd be honored to visit you again," he replied and Barbara threw her arms around his waist, giving him an air-snatching hug. This time, he returned the gesture, hugging her as if his own life depended on it. Never before had he felt the kindness and affection displayed by this woman, and he was reluctant to let it go; however, as much as he craved these "parents", there weren't his parents; nor was he here for them. He slowly detached himself from Barbara's embrace and stepped back. "It's been a privilege," he said softly, then turned and headed to the car.

"Thank you for everything," Melissa smiled, and then turned to trot after Alastair. "Are you okay?"

Alastair nodded, "Their question has me thinking, is all."

"About Arran's need of you?"

He nodded again, "When his fiancé appeared in my confessional and declared I had a brother in danger, the thought of why she'd come to me never even entered my mind. Didn't enter my mind until Arran's parents brought it up."

"All you could think about was the fact you had a brother you'd never met before and that that brother was in some sort of danger, I would have done the same as you."

"Seek out the brother?"

Melissa nodded, "And perhaps hope he could provide answers to this madness."

"Well, now that we have his general location, I'd say it's time to make Arran's acquaintance and sort out why it is that Jane flew halfway 'round the world to tell me about him and his alleged peril."

"You want me to drive this time?"

"Why?"

"You seem a mite bit agitated. Agitation and driving—never a good combination."

Alastair tossed her the keys, "Can't argue with sound reasoning. Besides, now that we know that Arran lives in Perth, I want to use your computer to do a Google search on him and his employer. See if anything comes up that will aide in our investigation."

Melissa arched her brow at him, then fired up the ignition, "You said *our*."

"Yes, I did. You going to deny that we're working this together? That I'm needed here?"

Melissa grinned, impressed by the man he was compared to the weeping mess he was on the day she met him. Of course, in all fairness, he'd only just witnessed a murder on that day. She certainly couldn't connect him with a dog collar. No wonder his faith was dying. "No, I'm not going to argue further. Since you've been in my company you've been less a hindrance."

CHAPTER SEVENTEEN

One Month Prior
Perth, Western Australia

"Why didn't you tell me?" Justin asked, plopping into a chair across from Jane's desk. Jane jumped, startled at the unexpected intrusion then lowered the lid on her laptop.

"Tell you what, Justin?" Jane asked calmly, as casually as she could muster; but her mind was doing somersaults. What had Justin discovered? She only prayed that, as good an investigator as he was, he hadn't turned up the connection between Arran and Rudd.

"That your fiancé works for Amherst Rudd," he echoed her thoughts, and Jane's heart sank. Justin was good, and when it came to his job, he was just as tenacious as she; which meant his life was now in as much danger as hers—if Rudd got wind that either of them was sniffing around in his affairs. She needed to distance his particular area of her investigation away from Rudd before he got ensnared.

"Because my fiancé's employment has nothing to do with locating his brother..."

"You're doing it again, Jane," Justin accused, leaning forward in his chair.

"Doing what, Justin?"

"Treating me like I'm dimwitted," Justin declared, narrowing his lips in frustration. "Should I remind you of our first conversation related to all of this? It won't be difficult to remind you since you know I have an eidetic memory."

"Eidetics relate to images...," Jane started to deflect, but Justin interrupted.

"Well, mine happens to relate to conversations. It's why I'm so good an investigator."

"Right, which is why you take so many notes...."

"*Arran is in trouble.*" Justin set to quoting, without looking at any notes. "*He's gotten himself mixed up in shady dealings with nefarious men—and I can't say who...yet. His brother may be his only hope of helping him—if we can find him in time. At least Arran seems to think he may be able to help. I won't know until I find him and question him."* Need I go on? If your fiancé works for Rudd and is in trouble, it doesn't take a math genius to connect those particular dots."

"I kept you out of it because I didn't want you to get hurt."

"Sure you didn't just want to keep that Walkley Award to yourself?"

"There won't be a Walkley Award. This is a personal investigation, being funded out of my own pocket. If you don't believe me, go talk to my editor. He'll tell you straight up that he's not condoned what I'm doing. In fact, he flat out told me that this paper will have none of it."

Justin leaned back and looked at Jane thoughtfully for a moment, "Okay, so if your brother is working for Rudd and has gotten himself entangled in something illegal, how is a priest in England supposed to help him?"

"Pardon?"

****

If you don't believe me, go talk to my editor. He'll tell you straight up that he's not condoned what I'm doing. In fact, he flat out told me that this paper will have none of it.

Okay, so if your brother is working for Rudd and has gotten himself entangled in something illegal, how is a priest in England supposed to help him?

Lachlan Dunne turned down the volume on the receiver and pulled his Samsung from his coat pocket. He dialed Amherst Rudd's direct line and within two rings was connected.

What do you know?

"You were right about her. She's persistent, that one. She hired an investigator to find Arran's brother in the hopes he'll be able to help Arran get out from beneath your employment, as it were; and from my prior eavesdropping, she plans to dig up dirt on you anyway she can..."

The only dirt dug will be to dig her grave.

"That the order boss?"

How certain are we that she's had no contact with her former fiancé?

"I'm as certain as lost virginity on a wedding night, boss. That girl has been so busy attempting to topple your organization that she hasn't been within sight of Arran Masters since the day he gave her the boot; and there's been no calls, texts, or emails either."

Unfortunately, she didn't believe the boot was a genuine dismissal. If she did, she'd have just moved on to the next tosser and washed her hands of Arran Masters immediately. Still, I'm glad that Arran is proving loyal. I'd hate to terminate his employment when we're within a few months of beginning our new enterprise. The Russian is certain he's nearing a viable product. It's just a matter of coordinating the distribution.

"So, do I have a termination notice to deliver?"

The last reporter that tried to snoop into my business came damned close to revealing things she ought not to. Got her nose lopped off for her efforts. I don't need another reporter with a burr up her butt stirring the pot. Deliver a warning first and if that doesn't work, deliver our final notice.

The line disconnected and Lachlan Dunne immediately knew what warning he would send their obstinate reporter. He turned over the ignition on his Holden Commodore and pulled onto the motorway, pointing the nose toward Arran's accounting offices.

CHAPTER EIGHTEEN

"Package for you, Miss Chaffin." The courier placed the package on the desk and handed over the clipboard to obtain the requisite signature. Jane scrawled her name onto the page and muttered a polite thanks. She reached for the small package, her brow knitted in confusion. She hadn't been expecting a special delivery.

She slid her fingernail along the tape and winced when it bent backwards. With a moan of pain, she popped the appendage into her mouth and then withdrew a pair of scissors from her desk drawer. After the throbbing stopped in her thumb, she proceeded to slit the tape.

The lid popped open, and she lay the scissors aside, pulling back the flaps all the way. Her heart immediately set to beating faster as she lifted a box, duplicate to the one her editor had received his warning in. Was she also receiving a warning, or was this box so generic as to be commonplace?

With dread pulsing through her veins, she drew in a deep breath through her nostrils and then lifted the small box from the larger one. She shoved aside the packaging and placed the small box on her desk, eyeing it suspiciously. After several, deep, calming breaths, she lifted the lid, and just as fast dropped it onto her desk, closing her eyes as the horror of its contents slammed into her brain. When she was certain she wouldn't throw up, she glanced back down into the box, tears pricking the corner of her eyes because she knew that she'd been the cause of the pain suffered.

She wanted to call out to any of the co-workers busily working at their desks, but didn't know precisely what they could do about it. Call the police? That certainly wouldn't be advisable. She also worried that drawing anyone else into this affair would lead to more deaths. No, she'd started this on her on, and she was going to have to continue on her own—with the exceptions of her boss and her investigator. She closed her eyes as a sudden wave of despair washed over her for drawing those two people into her personal quest to save her fiancé.

She drew in a deep, unsteady breath, suddenly immensely grateful that her behavior hadn't drawn the attention of her fellow reporters, all busily chasing their own leads.

She looked down in the box again and winced at its contents.

Dried blood stained each nail, which meant that the fingernails had been ripped from the nail bed, causing excruciating agony. Below the three blood-stained fingernails lay a small, folded piece of paper. She swiped the tears from her eyes and reached inside. Her hands were shaking as she gingerly reached around the contents and lifted the paper. One of the fingernails clung fast, the dried blood acting as an adhesive. She shook the paper, but the nail remained firmly affixed. With another deep breath to strengthen her resolve, she reached for her scissors and slid it beneath the nail, scraping the nail off the paper and back into the box. She closed her eyes as her stomach heaved. It took several more deep breaths before she felt courageous enough to open the paper.

Written in blood was a single word: *Arran*

"Oh God!"

Somehow Rudd had discovered her intent to investigate his businesses and was using Arran to keep her nose out of his affairs. Another shudder raced down her spine. How did he know? Was there someone in her circle of peers keeping an ear open for any mention of Rudd? But that didn't make sense, since she'd only mentioned her intent to investigate Rudd, her editor. Her breath stuck in her throat and she glanced toward his office. Could he be on Rudd's payroll? Is that why he was so adamant in attempting to deter her investigation? She shook the thought away. Oliver's distress over the loss of his last reporter was genuine and she couldn't see him hopping into bed with someone like Rudd, especially when it was obvious he feared and despised the man.

Perhaps the warning was simply to keep her in line? She sighed again, this time in relief. There wasn't a spy, rather Rudd just wanted to send her a message that even though Arran had dumped her, he still felt she could be a threat to his business. In that he was correct.

Still, if he could discern intent, then she'd never get anywhere near printing an exposé; and that meant she'd failed in her efforts to assist Arran long before she even started. Rudd simply had too many agents in too many organizations for her to be able to conduct an inquiry. *No wonder he's remained untouchable*, she thought.

Her gaze, blurred with tears, fell on the computer screen containing her limited notes thus far. She sniffed loudly as she honed in onto one bulleted point: *Alastair*

Was that the reason Arran had made it a point to tell her to give Alastair his regards? Not because he really wanted her to do so, rather because she knew that it was unlikely Rudd would be suspicious of someone outside of Australia? Was his parting comment a way of giving her a hint; that she should seek help outside of the country because Rudd was simply too connected within the country for anyone to be effective in toppling his enterprises?

Still, her investigator was correct—what could a priest in England possibly be capable of accomplishing? Did Arran even know the man's vocation? Was he simply hoping that someone elsewhere could provide assistance and his recent inquiry into locating his brother had popped to the forefront of his mind at a time of duress?

Perhaps there was more to Alastair than Arran was aware; something more than his priestly occupation.

"Yeah, like moonlighting as a constable?"

Without looking into the box again, she dropped the note back inside and quickly replaced the lid, sucking in a breath as a shudder raced through her body. The warning had deeply disturbed her, but more than anything it angered her. Angered her that she couldn't even come close to exposing Rudd; angered her that she was helpless in her attempts to aid Arran; and, mostly, she was angry that she couldn't even go to check on how Arran was faring after being subjected to torture—all because of her tenacious tendencies.

"I should let this go. Trust that Arran can get himself out of the mess he's gotten himself into; but if he could, he would have done.

He certainly wouldn't have dumped me the way he did if he thought he had a chance of leaving Rudd's employ."

She rubbed her eyes as a weary annoyance swept through her mind, "Arran, what have you gotten yourself wrapped up in, and how in God's name are we supposed to get you fired without you getting killed."

"You okay, Jane?"

The question startled Jane and she nearly toppled her chair when she righted too quickly.

"Sorry," her editor apologized, settling onto a chair beside her desk. "Want to tell me what has you so apparently jumpy? This anything to do with Rudd?"

Jane fought back the urge to cry, straightening her spine until her back threatened to go into spasms. She slid the box across the desk, but instead of picking it up or opening it as she thought he would, Oliver simply sat staring at it, his expression aghast.

"Aren't you the least bit curious?" Jane whispered sharply.

Oliver shook his head, his eyes pinned to the small container.

"It appears I've been warned off."

Oliver lifted his gaze then and speared her with an *I told you to drop it* look. "Let's take this somewhere private." His jaw clenched as he reached down and lifted the box from her desk.

Jane stood and walked stiffly toward her editor's office, but was too tense to sit. She heard the door click closed and immediately turned to face Oliver, who looked as if he'd witnessed a homicide.

"You look like I feel."

Oliver nodded, "I tried to tell you, Jane," he whispered harshly, dropping the box onto his desk. He looked at it a moment longer and then closed his eyes in dread, "Do I want to know its contents?"

"Rudd had one of his goons rip off three of Arran's fingernails," Jane replied unintentionally callous, and instantly regretted it when it looked as if her editor was going to faint. "Sit down, Oliver," she said, steering her friend to his chair.

"You realize," he murmured, "that if you don't let this go, you're going to disappear just as Amberly did. Do you really think I want to be receiving another late-night visit from Lachlan Dunne with a box containing one of your personal effects? Or worse, your fingernails?"

"I'm sorry I've put you center mass of this mess. I really am," Jane sighed, settling onto the chair in front of Oliver's desk, "but how can I stop now when Arran is in danger?"

Just then, Jane's mobile rang, interrupting their conversation. She pulled it from her pocket, glanced at the incoming caller information, and then swiped to unlock the screen, "Justin? I wasn't expecting..."

Jane! It's me, Justin!

"Yes, I know," Jane responded, wondering if he could hear her. "I was just saying..."

Jane, I'm in trouble!

Jane sat silent, waiting. Something was off about the call, and while she was concerned for her investigator's well-being, she couldn't shake the weird feeling that settled over her. She didn't wait long to have her concerns validated.

They said that if you don't come, they'll kill me. Come to the causeway. Someone will meet you there.

Again, she waited, refusing to respond as might be anticipated; yet the caller appeared to respond to that which she may have asked.

Don't ask why, Jane. They said they won't hurt you. They just want to talk. Please Jane, I don't want to die.

The call disconnected. Jane pulled the phone away from her ear and stared at it for a moment longer before whispering, "Justin's dead."

"What did you say, Jane? Who was on the phone?" Oliver asked, but Jane didn't answer. Instead she pulled a notepad over and yanked a pen up, scribbling quickly. She then turned the pad around and waited.

Oliver read what she'd written, sucking in a sharp breath at what it said:

Justin's dead. If we're going to discuss anything more, we need to leave this office. It's bugged.

CHAPTER NINETEEN

"How do you know Justin's dead?" Oliver asked the moment they exited the building. "And who in Hell is Justin anyway? And how do you know the office is bugged? And where precisely are we going?"

Jane's jawed was clinched in fury, so it took her a moment to relax enough to be able to speak, but when she did, the words fell out in a tumble of anxiety, "I surmise the call was a recorded message. Justin's phone was dialed to call me with instructions to meet for a chat, but though it was Justin's voice, it was automated. He didn't respond to my initial queries, just kept speaking as if I *were* responding, which I stopped doing early on in the conversation.

Anyway, Justin was the man I hired to assist in my investigation of Rudd, only he wasn't actually investigating Rudd, rather helping to locate Arran's brother; only, he knew that the investigation was directly related to Rudd, and the only way that Rudd would know of his involvement at all was to bug our offices. Initially, I dismissed that as a possibility; thought instead we could have a spy in our midst. Then I dismissed that and thought that the warning I received— Arran's fingernails—was just that—a warning to not get involved. Then in your office when Justin called, the possibility the offices are bugged became more than an assumption, rather a high probability.

As to why they would kill him, I can only guess that he's a damned good investigator and they didn't want either of us continuing this inquiry. Basically, by hiring him, I got him murdered. As to where we're headed? To the pub. I need a pint."

They picked up Jane's car from the parking structure, then headed down Stirling. A few minutes later, Jane pulled into the parking lot of the One Night Shag pub. The bartender immediately called out to Jane upon her entering, "Pint for ye?"

Jane nodded and settled on a stool in the corner.

"And for ye're friend? What'll 'e have, mate?"

"A pint also," Oliver replied and sat down on the stool next to Jane. "You a regular here?" He asked while they awaited their brew.

Jane nodded again. She'd fallen silent since her emotional diatribe, her thoughts a jumble, but Oliver's query had her cocking her eyebrow in question, ceasing the barrage of worry tumbling about her head.

"Was it wise to come here then?" Oliver queried softly, glancing about at the patrons engaged in conversations with friends or potential lovers.

"What do you mean?" Jane asked, following his gaze around the room.

"If Rudd is keeping tabs on you, it's a fair bet he'll know your regular haunts. And if he means to do you harm, you'll certainly make it easier for him by visiting those regular haunts, don't you think?"

"I get your meaning, yes," Jane replied soberly, "but I'm not leaving here until I've finished my beer. I'm in dire need."

"Jane, what are you going to do?" Oliver asked as soon as the bartender deposited their mugs in front of them and walked away. "I think maybe the reason that Rudd is sending you warnings right now is he's trying to keep from killing you; and if that's the case, don't you think it would be in your best interest to heed those warnings? You won't do Arran any good if you're dead."

"And I apparently am doing him no good alive either. If Rudd knew everything, he'd realize that we're not getting very far in our investigations, so why..."

"Kill off your investigator so early?" Oliver concluded, reading her thoughts.

"Yeah. You'd think he'd be satisfied that sending Arran's fingernails would suffice as a warning."

"But it didn't, remember? The call to your mobile came after you stated that you didn't intend to stop investigating. Right after in fact, which would lend credence to your suspicion that the offices are bugged. They probably killed your investigator because they knew you relied on his abilities. You said he was good, yeah?"

"Yeah, and Rudd must have already captured him and coerced that recording from him as a contingency against my not taking the fingernail warning. But then that means they must have killed him before they even knew I'd not drop it. Otherwise why not just have him call…"

"You said it. They probably figured best to eliminate at least one threat in the hopes that you'd not keep at it. They probably intended to lure you to that meeting as *requested* in the recording only as a contingency against you not heeding the first warning. Intended to let you live initially, but now…"

"Now I'm a threat, unless I drop it. What a mess."

"Well, I may not know everything, but I do know that you'll definitely be next unless they become suddenly very satisfied that you have absolutely zero interest in Rudd; and that you'll stop trying to save your fiancé from his clutches."

"How can I, Oliver? How can I walk away from Arran when he's obviously in trouble? What kind of person could do that?"

"One who wants to live?" Oliver quipped humorlessly, then downed the remainder of his beer. "Come on, let's find somewhere you're less known to finish this chat."

Jane downed her drink and tossed a five onto the countertop. Oliver did likewise and then they both moved back out onto the walkway, standing in indecision for a moment.

"Fancy a walk along the waterfront?" Oliver asked.

Jane shook her head, "I think I'll head home…"

"Damn it, Jane! Have you bollocks for brains, girl? If you don't show up at the causeway fairly soon, it's fair certain your flat is the first place…"

"Calm yourself, Oliver. I'm only stopping by long enough to collect a suitcase…and my passport. Tonight I'll book a motel room, but tomorrow I intend to book a flight to England."

"Oh, Jane, I fear for you. Must you be so pig-headed?"

"If it were Nancy…"

Oliver put up a hand to silence her, "I'd be on a plane to England." He concluded, wrapping his arms around her and hugging her tight. "Just tell me you're certain that this trip will help."

"I wish I could, but this is the only avenue I know to take to get help for Arran. Any other way will be easily discovered by Rudd." She pulled from his embrace. "I have to try. I don't know Alastair, but Arran felt certain that help would have to come from outside our borders, and he's the only name I've got."

"Okay, you go get packed and get out of that flat as fast as you can throw some things in a bag. I'll walk back to the office and retrieve my car."

"I can run you over."

Oliver shook his head, ushering her toward her car, "The longer it takes you to clear out of that flat, the more time Rudd will have to find you. Even taking five minutes to run me back to the office is five minutes you don't have to spare. Now go. And contact me as soon as you're settled."

"What are you going to do about the bugs in the office?"

"I'll have the offices swept and the bugs removed. I can't guarantee they won't be able to get bugs in there again…"

"Looks like bug-sweeping will be something needed daily."

"They'll just find another way to find out what you're up to."

"Perhaps, or perhaps without the bugs in the office, Rudd will become deaf and blind to my movements and I can do what's needed to destroy him."

Oliver sighed heavily and shook his head, "You aren't naïve enough to believe that."

Jane smiled sadly, "No, I'm not, which is why I'm getting on that plane. He can't stop me if I'm in England. Take care, Oliver. I'll be back soon."

Jane pulled her keys from her pocket, placed a kiss on her boss's cheek, and then sprinted for her car. Oliver was right, she needed to pack and get out of sight fast, or her attempts to help Arran would end in her death tonight.

Oliver watched her pull away before heading for his own vehicle. He hoped she'd be safe in another country, but something deep inside told him that as long as she continued to dig into Rudd's affairs, the quicker she'd be digging her own grave.

CHAPTER TWENTY

Oliver pulled into the parking structure of the newspaper office at six the following morning, relief flooding his entire being. Jane had called the night before with much-needed news that she was still breathing.

I'm staying at the...

"Don't tell me, Jane. If Rudd comes looking for you..."

It's best you have nothing to tell, I get it. I just wish Rudd wasn't so desperate to end me.

"He doesn't stay out of prison by allowing reporters free rein to snoop into his affairs. You should know this, Jane. I warned you about what happens to nosy reporters."

I was thinking about all of this while I was packing. I don't think Rudd's interest in me has to with Arran at all. I think you won the prize with what you just said—it has to do with my wanting to investigate him. My motives are to free Arran from his employ; Rudd's is to prevent exposure.

"So, just convince him you'll drop..."

We've been over this, Oliver. I can't just leave Arran in the grasp of a maniacal lunatic. If you saw how despondent Arran was when he left Rudd's offices the day he gave me the shaft. He isn't happy about whatever arrangements Rudd has forced him into. And do you really think that Rudd would be convinced I wouldn't say anything?

"Probably not. You still going to England? Shit...I shouldn't have asked that."

Don't worry over it. I know we're being extremely cautious, but I don't think Rudd has managed to bug our phones. So, I'm leaving tomorrow afternoon. I'm going to find Alastair, see if he has any ideas on how to bring down Rudd.

"From...well, you know. You also know how insane that sounds?"

Well, we can't do it from within Australia. Rudd has too many connections that protect his interests. I can't see anyone somewhere else having an interest in Rudd's affairs.

"Precisely, which is why no one would have an interest in assisting you."

No one but Alastair—possibly.

Oliver sighed, "You're a stubborn one, Jane. Find a way to keep me informed, will you? I will take a bend on one knee tonight that someone above will watch over you; keep you safe."

If you're going to be doing any kneeling, I'd prefer you request that Alastair have connections out the wazoo that will finish Rudd once and for all.

"Goodnight, Jane."

Goodnight, Oliver. Don't worry too much. I know I'll feel safer getting off Australian soil; out of Rudd's reach.

****

Lachlan Dunne was fuming. He'd never had someone ignore his warnings. He couldn't hear both sides of the conversation going on because Oliver Carter was obviously speaking into his mobile; however, from his one-sided conversation, it was easy to discern to whom he was speaking—Jane Chaffin; and it was equally easy to discern that she had zero interest in dropping her investigation into his boss's affairs. He was just glad that he'd determined to place a bug in both Oliver Carter and Jane Chaffin's cars, or he might never have known her intent. He picked up his phone and dialed Rudd.

What's the word?

"Arran's fiancé didn't heed the warning. She's flying out to England sometime this afternoon to try to find help in her quest."

"Take care of her before she leaves then."

"I don't know where she is. The man who was supposed to be watching her place…well, he apparently arrived *after* she managed to gather her belongings and hide herself at a motel somewhere. The only chance would be to nab her at the airport before she boards. Highly likely we'd be successful.

Then I take it you'll be flying out also?

"I will, yes, but I need to overnight a package to a postal service in England. Make certain I have the tools needed to take care of business."

I'll expect good news upon your return.

"You'll have it."

CHAPTER TWENTY-ONE

Melissa and Alastair sat outside of Adelaide Terrace just watching the people coming and going; neither seemed in a hurry to get out of the car.

"It's as if...I don't know." Melissa had always been confident in her abilities, but now she felt

"You worried that the minute we head inside, we could find ourselves with a target on our backs?"

"Yeah, especially since we don't know precisely what Arran is mixed up in."

"He's the victim in all of this."

"Yeah or he could be the perp, which means he could be the one to put the target on our backs, if he finds out I'm a DS."

Alastair shook his head, "Jane said he was in danger..."

"That doesn't make him innocent, Alastair. He could be in danger because his boss found him out."

"If we'd have called and spoken with him first..."

"You're assuming we had the time to do so. Remember, Jane died trying to get help for Arran, purportedly. If he is a victim in this, time is of the essence. If he's the perp and we called him ahead of time and revealed anything at all, he could have said, "Yeah, come on down under for a visit..." and had us killed immediately."

"Either way, how are we supposed to handle this? If he's in trouble, do we tell him what's transpired..."

"Best to wait to ascertain his involvement before letting on to anything. That way we may just be able to allay suspicion long enough to collect evidence."

"What do we tell him about Jane?"

"Nothing...yet."

"Then how do we explain our sudden presence here? What if he knows that Jane went to England..."

"We can sit here and play what ifs all day. Our best course is to just say we discovered your brother…somehow…we'll figure that out later. After we get answers to his involvement…"

"Well, the only way we're going to get answers is to get out of this car. If it does turn out that he's the cause of all of this pain, then we…what? Arrest him? He isn't the one who killed Jane."

"That we know of. Look, I'm a DS, which means I'm here to get answers related to the murder of Jane Chaffin. The only thing is, I can't investigate via the normal routes because those are closed to me here. So, we go in using your suggestion."

"Visiting?"

"Yeah, but I can't be a police officer. That will look too suspicious, especially if Amherst Rudd is behind Jane's death. I don't think Arran's brother, with a police officer in tow, would be believed as a mere visit."

"You're my fiancé," Alastair offered, a little too rapidly if Melissa's raised brow were an indicator.

"And our ruse for making a sudden visit to a man for whom we had absolutely no knowledge of until this week?"

"The truth?"

"Pardon?"

"I know we don't want to reveal too much too soon, but if we stick close to the truth then we won't get tangled up in a lie. We tell him that Jane sought me out in England, but before we could get to know her…well…you know."

"Do you think he knows about her demise?"

Alastair shook his head, "Not unless he's responsible…"

"Or the one responsible confessed his culpability, which is highly unlikely; so, we should approach this as if Arran is innocent and unaware of his fiancé's death."

"Right," Alastair agreed and then drew in a deep breath. "Ready?"

"As is humanly possible," Melissa replied, drawing in her own deep breath. "Quite frankly, I've never felt so discombobulated and unprepared for anything in my life."

"Me either."

"Okay, let's do this."

They both stepped out of their vehicle, just as a car pulled into the lot; and there was no mistaking the man who stepped from the vehicle. It was Arran Masters.

CHAPTER TWENTY-TWO

Arran spotted them the moment he stepped from his vehicle also. They all just stood there, staring.

Barbara and Tim Masters confirmed that Alastair and Arran were twins, but to come face-to-face with someone who looked exactly the same was more than a little disconcerting. Had they been aware of each other prior, the disconcertion would not have been present, but these men were strangers; no more than a paper knowledge of the other existed.

Arran snapped out of his daze first, walking rapidly toward the couple, still standing and staring transfixed. Melissa, already in awe of Alastair's attractiveness was rendered breathless at having two men, identical in distinguished beauty, in such close proximity, yet unable to do more than disrobe them in her mind.

"Alastair?" Arran asked the moment he stopped in front of the man. His gaze raked Alastair's features, then stopped when his gaze encountered Alastair's eyes. "Different colored eyes, but the same man."

Alastair's inability to respond, jarred Melissa from her shocked silence and she stepped forward, extending her hand in greeting, "Hello, I'm Melissa. You'll have to forgive Alastair. When Jane came and found us in England, we were more than a little skeptical about Alastair having an identical twin."

Arran tore his gaze away from Alastair and stared at the woman who'd addressed him, shaking her proffered hand, "A pleasure to meet you...I didn't catch your name."

"Melissa, Alastair's fiancé, and the pleasure is ours. It's hard to imagine Alastair so quiet right now. He's been extremely animated about the prospect of having a brother and very determined to fly down to meet that brother..."

"I'm just in shock, Melissa," Alastair replied softly, smiling gently.

"So, Jane found you," Arran snorted softly. "I hoped that she would catch the clue I tossed at her, but never imagined she'd go flying across the globe the locate you."

"Clue?" Alastair queried.

Arran shrugged, "Not important. I shouldn't be surprised. Tenacious reporter, that girl. What did she say to get you on a plane anyway?"

"That you're in danger," Alastair blurted out and Arran's eyes went wide.

"Whatever made her jump to that conclusion?" Arran asked rhetorically. "I simply told her to give my regards to Alastair...after I unceremoniously ended our long-term relationship," he concluded, his cheeks turning a deep scarlet from embarrassed remembrance.

"And you didn't think she'd infer that you're in some sort of trouble?" Melissa asked, trying mightily not to sound like a trained interrogator. "She obviously interpreted your message that way or she wouldn't have hopped a plane to Leeds. Are you in trouble?"

"I...um...," Arran mumbled, obviously attempting to think of how to broach his current difficulties. After a minute, he continued, "I wanted her to know that I hadn't broken up with her because I wanted to, rather because I didn't have a choice; and, yes, I admit that I wanted her to know..." Arran sighed. "I wish I could thank her for finding you, but if I go anywhere near her..."

"Why don't we go inside, and you can tell us what's going on and what we can do to help. That's why we're here."

"If we want to speak in private, we're going to have to go for a drive...oh no!" Arran's face drained of all color and he drew a deep breath in through his nostrils.

Alastair and Melissa turned to follow Arran's panicked gaze and their own gazes widened. Walking determinedly toward them was a bulldog of a man, and he seemed very displeased with Arran.

"Who've we 'ere, Arran?" Lachlan Dunne asked, trying to sound amiable; but despite the amicable tone, Arran couldn't quite find his voice, so Alastair stretched out a hand in greeting.

"Hello, I'm Alastair."

"British?" Lachlan asked, his tone oddly accusatory.

"That's right. And you are?"

"Curious as to why you look so much like my mate Arran here."

"He's my brother..."

"You never told us you had a brother, Arran," Lachlan quipped pleasantly, but that accusatory tone remained.

"I didn't know I had a brother, Lachlan. Not until recently," Arran replied, trying to keep the hostility from his tone. A tone not lost on Melissa and Alastair, nor was the name used.

Melissa's eyes widened slightly. Could this be Lachlan Dunne, Amherst Rudd's enforcer? The man whom, she alleged, had flown to England to murder Jane on British soil?

"How do you not know you have a brother?"

"The world's a big place," Melissa offered.

"My fiancé and I are on vacation here in Perth," Alastair interjected. "Melissa spotted my doppelgänger and was so taken aback that we followed the poor chap, only to discover he's my long-lost twin brother." Alastair improvised, forgetting their plan to be honest as to how they'd discovered Arran's existence.

"Well, fancy that!" Lachlan exclaimed, his tone disbelieving. "And the beautiful woman your sister?"

"I'm sorry, but I thought I just said that she's my fiancé," Alastair interjected possessively, moving to grasp Melissa's hand. The way in which this potential murderer was eyeing her made his hackles raise. "Arran was just about to take us for a drive so we can get acquainted. It was lovely to meet you, Lachlan. Perhaps we can all dine together some time," Alastair said politely, extending his hand; his tone effectively ending the interaction.

Lachlan nodded, grasping the hand firmly. It was just like a scene from a movie in which the stronger attempts to intimidate the weaker by squeezing his hand too firmly; and the weaker attempting to pretend the bones in his hand aren't being crushed to dust.

Lachlan grinned wickedly at Alastair's resolve and finally released his grip, taking a step back.

"We'll do dinner and I'll be seeing you later, Arran," he concluded, leaving no doubt that a long, informational-gathering chat was in Arran's near future. Arran, emotionally rattled, nodded and then motioned for Alastair and Melissa to load up in the couple's rental.

Lachlan watched them pull from the car park and then dialed his boss.

Yeah, what is it?

"Our boy, Arran, has an identical twin brother, who just happened to decide to visit—from Leeds, England. I'm certain that's the brother that Jane Chaffin sent that investigator to locate."

What are you thinking?

"Well, there's no doubting he's the brother, but the timing of the trip is too coincidental for me."

Think he knows anything?

"I can't say if Jane managed to reveal anything before I shut her up. If they didn't know anything, why jump a plane to Australia so soon after Jane's sudden departure from this earth? Could be the brother was really eager to meet Arran, but if he knew about Arran and jumped a plane to meet him, why the ruse about happenstance? Why lie and say their meeting was by chance?" Lachlan was thinking aloud, but Rudd wasn't interested in his suppositions, only potential threats to himself.

Think they can cause trouble?

"I don't know. I'd have to know if they know anything before I can ascertain the threat level."

Got their names?

"I didn't make a note of them, but I got the rental car information, so it won't be too difficult getting their names."

Do it, and then find out the connection to anything Jane Chaffin may have relayed to them.

"Consider it done."

And Lachlan?

"Yeah, boss?"

If it becomes necessary, arrange a meeting with me.

"Understood."

CHAPTER TWENTY-THREE

"That was one disturbing fellow," Alastair commented as soon as they pulled onto the Kwinana Freeway. Alastair didn't have the first notion of where they were going, he just took the first freeway access and depressed the pedal to the floorboard. His nerves were still jumping after their encounter with whom he assumed was Jane's murderer. His nerves were also having a hard time calming since he knew he had to reveal that information to Arran.

"Take the next exit. There's a café where we can relax and talk."

"Talk, yes. Relax? Not so certain," Alastair responded, the tension in his tone prevalent.

Melissa sensed the tightness in his voice and placed a hand in reassurance on his shoulder, "Try not to worry overly much."

"How long have you been engaged?" Arran asked, eyeing the gesture with envy. He wished Jane could be there to support and comfort him.

"We're not," Melissa answered, and Alastair jerked his head to glare at her.

"We agreed..."

"I know, but I think we can safely assume that your brother is indeed in trouble and not the one pulling the strings to all of this mayhem. Besides, I'm not certain how convincingly we can continue it without slipping up. Remember your ridiculous outburst about seeing your doppelgänger? Nerves are affecting our ability to think straight, much less keep a cover story straight. The fewer people we need to lie to, the easier it'll be to get through this."

"Would someone mind explaining?" Arran asked, his brow knitted.

"Let's settle in with a drink first," Melissa replied as Alastair found a spot in the parking lot. "Personally, I could use one."

"I second that," Arran replied, climbing from the back seat of the car.

Within a few minutes they were settled into a booth at the back of the café, away from the bustle of the crowd. Each ordered a lager.

"I didn't know priests were allowed to drink," Melissa quipped and Arran's eyes bulged.

"You're a priest?" He spat, nearly choking on a Brazil nut.

Alastair nodded solemnly, "Melissa is well aware of my intent to leave the order."

"Why? You aren't one of *those* priests, are you? Get in trouble..."

It was Alastair's turn to choke on a nut. He coughed up the obstruction, shaking his head all the while.

"I think he's trying to convey that he's not a pedophile," Melissa grinned and Alastair nodded rapidly.

"If I'd known you were a priest, I never would have given Jane that clue. Still, I'm glad you're here. Maybe while you're here, you can stop by her apartment and give her a message for me. I can't go anywhere near her. Of course, I'm assuming she flew back at the same time...what? Why the looks?"

"Tell us why Jane translated your clue to give Alastair regards to mean you're in trouble. We think we know it has to do with Amherst Rudd. That *was* his thug, Lachlan Dunne, yeah?" Melissa stated, this time not attempting to hide the official tone.

"You sound like a copper," Arran deflected.

Melissa reached inside her pocket and pulled out her badge, "I am. I'm DS Melissa Lloyd."

"Dear sweet Jesus, would someone explain..."

"Jane is dead, Arran," Alastair interjected softly, not wanting him to hear it in an official capacity from Melissa. He continued the explanation in a rush, "She showed up at my church, in my confessional. She was determined to tell me that you—my brother— a brother of whom I had no knowledge—was in trouble. I still don't know what she thought I could accomplish..."

"Any attempt to investigate Rudd within Australian borders doesn't bode well for the investigator. I gave her your name in the hopes someone outside Australia could help me, but, Jesus, I had no idea you were a priest. How did she...die?" He choked on the last word, trying hard to maintain his composure. His Jane, his precious

Jane was dead, and it was his fault. He'd broken up with her in the hopes of protecting her from this very fate; and had he not given her that clue…he shook his head. Something deep inside told him that she'd have ended with the same fate whether he'd mentioned Alastair or not. He wasn't exaggerating when he'd called her tenacious, and his dismissal of her, with little explanation, had most likely set off her journalistic radar. She'd have immediately set about trying to discover why and would have found out it had to do with Rudd. The minute he'd been forced into Rudd's illegal enterprises, he'd sealed her fate. He swiped at the tear that escaped. "What happened?" He reiterated firmly when neither answered his first query.

"We don't have much more than circumstantial evidence right now, but it would seem that Lachlan Dunne stabbed her inside your brother's confessional," Melissa supplied.

"Dunne?" Arran's gaze widened.

Melissa nodded, "My initial investigation showed him flying in to Leeds shortly after Jane and flying out the day after her demise. That's why we're here. My boss determined that I needed to be here to prove his involvement. Find a way to connect him to the murder. Maybe find a way to connect his employer too."

"I'll kill the son-of-a-bitch," Arran growled.

"At least wait until I've proven his guilt," Melissa advised.

"If Rudd finds out who you really are, and the true purpose of your…"

"That's why we're hoping to continue posing as a couple, at least if we encounter Dunne again…" Alastair interjected.

"We most definitely will."

"Well, maybe by acting like we're just a couple visiting, we can head off suspicion and find the evidence needed to arrest Dunne. I really am sorry about Jane, Arran."

"You need to get on the next plane to Leeds," Arran said firmly, swiping at another tear and sniffing loudly. "Rudd isn't going to believe that you and your fiancé just happened to fly to Australia shortly after *my* fiancé flew to England seeking help to destroy his business. He's a suspicious man. So much so, he's watching my movements and associations like a hawk. At least until he can assure himself that I'm not a risk to his business; until he's assured of my loyalty. Do you know what will happen to you if he discovers you're a DS; that you're here to investigate him?"

"Does it involve acid?" Melissa tried to keep her tone unaffected by the prospect that she could be subjected to torture sometime in the near future; remembering what her boss told her about how Rudd's enemies disappear.

The color drained from Arran's face as he recalled the teenage boy suffering that exact fate. The screams and the smell made him queasy again.

"Drink something before you pass out," Melissa demanded, pushing the lager toward Arran's hand. Arran picked up his mug and downed the remainder of his brew. "You don't look good either," Melissa continued, speaking to Alastair who'd also lost the color in his face at the mention of acid, "so drink something." Alastair complied mechanically. "Listen, the only way to stop Dunne and Rudd is to find proof Dunne's visit to Leeds was to commit murder at Rudd's behest. To do that, I need to find his knife. Test it for blood residue."

"He carries a beastly blade attached to his person all of the time. I don't know how you'll get it off him—if that's even the weapon he used. And what makes you think that there'll be any residue to test? You don't actually believe he kills and then doesn't clean his blade."

"Unless he cleans it in bleach or other harsh cleansers, there's the potential of finding blood somewhere—on the handle or blade...ah, shit. Maybe just matching his blade to the wound. Look, I'm not in forensics! I know that bringing Dunne to justice is as likely to succeed as a man walking on the moon without a space suit, but I've somehow convinced my superior that it's worth my coming here to try. What I really need to do..."

"What are we supposed to do, Melissa?" Alastair interrupted. "I'm just a priest...former priest..."

"And I'm a police officer," Melissa rejoined sharply. "This is what I do—bring the bad guys to justice..."

"Not alone, I'd wager," Alastair snapped back, fire in his eyes. It made Melissa want to rip his clothes off right there. Instead she drew in a deep breath to steady her calm.

"Not alone, no, and I'll admit to feeling like a babe in the woods. I haven't the first clue how to proceed."

"You need to get out of Australia," Arran reiterated.

"You come with us," Alastair offered, his tone turning desperate.

"I can't. I leave and Rudd will send Dunne to finish me off just like he did Jane..."

"That's it! That's what we'll do!" Melissa exclaimed suddenly, slapping her hand on the table. Both men gawked, not getting her sudden enthusiasm at placing Arran in more danger. Melissa stared back, wondering why neither got that enthusiasm, "Ah, come on, it's as obvious as you two are handsome."

Both men's brow quirked simultaneously.

"Look, if we can hint that you're fleeing Rudd's vicinity, he may think you're ready to reveal what you know and send Dunne to silence you."

"Yeah, we got that much," Alastair replied unenthusiastically.

Melissa sighed, "If I can get back to home ground, bring Dunne to us, I can ensnare him. That will be safer than trying to find evidence down here with Rudd's other men ready to jump into the fray and potentially kill us all."

"I don't have a passport," was all Arran could mutter, and that was unexcitedly.

"How long?"

"Three-to-six weeks," Arran replied in anticipation of her question. "If I put a rush on it."

"Damn," Melissa snapped.

"Yeah," Arran lamented, "and if you think I'd be able to apply for one without Rudd finding it out, then you're the daftest DS I've ever met."

"Why are you so important?" Alastair asked abruptly. "Why was Jane? What threat are you to him? What threat was Jane?"

"Good questions." Melissa was impressed that he'd thought of them; wondering why she hadn't. Her focus was Dunne and trying to discover a way to bring him to justice for Jane's murder. The whys of it all were secondary to her at this juncture. "Maybe you can apply for the force, since you aren't donning your collar anymore."

"Too old," Alastair replied offhandedly.

Arran sighed heavily, leaning back against the bench. The waitress came over to ask about refills and they decided to order some dinner. When she departed, Arran started his explanations.

"I'm Rudd's accountant."

"Yeah, we know, but...ah, damn," Alastair muttered, automatically jumping to the conclusion that Rudd was completely crooked, which meant his brother wasn't exactly a saint if he worked for a crook. It was an assumption Arran corrected.

"Rudd has legit enterprises too. So many, in fact, that I was unaware that he had illegal enterprises at all. I was the lead accountant for his legit businesses."

Melissa brow quirked, "So then..."

"...why would he put me under such scrutiny?" Arran concluded the query. Melissa nodded, and Arran sighed again, "Because recently I was *persuaded* to begin working in his illegal enterprises. He had a lead accountant already in place, but...well, I don't know the buts. I only know that the other accountant went missing. No doubt sowed seeds of distrust in Rudd's head which didn't bode well for him."

"Sounds as if Rudd's a very suspicious man," Alastair commented thoughtfully.

Arran cradled his hand, three fingers of which were wrapped in gauze, "He hasn't remained in the position he has by being trusting, no."

"He do that to you?" Melissa nodded at the bandages. "Do anything else to hurt you?

"Besides murder the only woman I've ever loved?" Arran snapped harshly, then looked down at the bandages. "He sent Dunne to remove three of my fingernails. I don't know why, but maybe as a way of drilling it into my head that I'm a part of something now that I'd better get on board with one hundred percent."

"So he's keeping tabs on you because you now know he's dirty?" Melissa asked.

"Downright muddy, and yes, that's why he's keeping tabs on me. To ensure I keep my mouth shut; to ensure I don't plan to reveal what I know to the authorities. Once I've proven myself loyal, he'll call off the hounds. Anyway, if I'd known just how crooked he was, I would have left well enough alone and not sent Jane off to get murdered. I was trying to protect her; distance her from me, since my hands are dirty now too. Stubborn, beautiful, wonderful Jane. She knew how much I loved her and wouldn't believe I would just dump her like I did. She knew something wasn't right, and I wasn't a good enough actor to pretend everything was okay. If I were, I could have kept the relationship and kept Jane in the dark. But it's been eating at me ever since Rudd forced me into that position, and I knew Jane would catch on fast by my demeanor. I killed her any way you twist it. And it won't be long before he finds out your true reason for "visiting" a brother you didn't know you even had until Jane flew to Leeds. By coming here, you've pretty much guaranteed an acid bath for yourselves."

All three fell silent when the waitress delivered their meals. They started eating by rote; each contemplating their fate. Melissa knew that Arran was right—eventually Rudd would discover their intent and send his henchmen to stop their inquiries.

Alastair wondered what he'd gotten himself into. Never in his wildest imaginings had he realized how different life outside the church could be.

Arran sat musing over his fate. Would Rudd think he'd brought the police from Leeds in and decide to sever their relationship—permanently?

Arran pushed his plate aside, covered his face with his hands and started to weep softly. Alastair reached a hand across, but Melissa stopped him from touching Arran, "Let him have a moment."

After a few minutes, the sounds of sobbing lessened.

"Arran, I know this is exceedingly difficult for you, but if you could just hold it together until we get you out from under this mess?" Melissa asked compassionately.

Arran lifted his head and rubbed his eyes vigorously. "Where are you staying?" He questioned suddenly, his voice thick with emotion. "I'd invite you to stay with me, but we'd have to monitor every word..."

"If you have room, staying with you might prove advantageous," Melissa chimed in. "I'm assuming Rudd has your apartment bugged?" Arran nodded, and Melissa continued. "We may be able to use that to our advantage. Make it seem as if we're genuinely visiting; catching up. If we can convince your employer we have nothing to hide, that we aren't here for anything other than a reunion, I may be able to conduct my investigation under the radar, without arousing suspicions; and Rudd may just decide to call off the hounds."

"Yeah, or they may discover our real reason for being here and know precisely where to locate us," Alastair retorted.

Arran sighed loudly, "I have a spare room you can share, and it would be nice to get to know my brother better. We can keep our conversations at the apartment innocuous and discuss the investigation outside, as we're doing now. I'm in agreement with Melissa. And yes, I will do everything I can to regain and maintain my composure until we see this through."

Melissa and Arran nodded solemnly, both wondering just how any of them were going to see this through. Melissa dialed the motel room she'd booked earlier and cancelled.

****

Lachlan Dunne pulled open the door to the car rental agency and strolled in cockily, grinning widely when the proprietor's eyes widened in recognition. Dunne loved the rock-star feeling of fame simply for being Rudd's right-hand man. Wherever he went, people cowered in fear at his approach and catered to his every whim on command. He felt he'd earned his Prima Donna of Hitmen status and reveled in the notoriety.

"Morning," he said amicably, leaning on the countertop in feigned relaxation. "Need your help, mate."

"Certainly, Mr. Dunne," the young man replied quickly and Dunne wanted to laugh. The poor chap had probably tinkled in his trousers already, just by his being there. His ego elevated another notch.

Dunne reached in his pant pocket and retrieved the license plate number he'd scribbled on a scrap piece of paper, "I need the name of the person who rented this car." He slid the paper over.

The proprietor glanced at it and then punched the number into his database—GA 5452, "It was rented to a Melissa Lloyd out of Leeds, England."

"Anything on her passenger?"

"No, Mr. Dunne. We aren't required to list the names of passengers, only the driver."

"Was she required to give a copy of her car license?"

"Um, well, um, yes." The proprietor was suddenly fearful of where this inquiry was headed. Dunne stopped short of asking for a copy, but cocked his brow as if expecting it to be offered, which the proprietor did with immediacy, fearing more for his life than a citation. "I'll, um, print off a copy?" He inquired softly, hoping Dunne would decline the offer. He didn't. The proprietor located the document and hit the print button, sweat popping out on his upper lip as he prayed no one would discover the illegality of his actions.

Dunne took the proffered copy and nodded, turning to leave the car rental agency. He pulled his phone from his coat pocket and dialed his boss.

What have you discovered? Rudd asked as soon as he answered his phone.

"One of our visitors is Melissa Lloyd."

Is that supposed to mean something?

"I don't know yet. I'm going to ring over to police headquarters to have them do a search. If she *is* here just visiting with Arran's identical brother, then nothing suspicious will turn up."

You know what to do if something suspicious does turn up.

CHAPTER TWENTY-FOUR

As they strolled across the car park toward Arran's apartment building, Melissa reiterated the importance of maintaining a believable façade within Arran's apartment, "We cannot let on the reason for our being here; nor that we are doing anything other than traveling."

"We understand the risk, Melissa," Alastair stated softly, the tenor in his voice betraying his nervousness; a behavior Melissa readily pointed out.

"You're going to have to control your speech, Alastair. You give too much away when your nervous tone comes out."

"I was a priest, not an actor; and I'm certainly not used to being in harm's way."

"If you could converse angrily for our entire trip, you'd manage to pull it off, since that anger dispels your nervousness. As it is, I warned you how dangerous this could be; I told you to stay away from my investigation..."

"I am well aware that this is my fault," Alastair rejoined loudly, anger blazing in his gaze when he stopped and turned his anger full bear towards her. "I am also aware that I could not sit by with my brother's life in jeopardy..."

"A brother you didn't even know existed prior to a few days ago!"

"Family is still family!"

"And this family has more than a few issues," Arran interrupted, gazing about to ensure their spectacle hadn't drawn unwanted attention. "I'd say let's take this inside, but if you two persist in yelling about the real reason you're here, Rudd's henchmen are going to be here within half hour to dispatch us all."

Melissa and Alastair glared at each other a moment longer and then Melissa glanced away, drawing in a deep breath. "Sorry for the row, Arran. I think that Alastair and I are just tense because we're treading in deep water without benefit of life preservers. It doesn't help any that your life is in jeopardy also, just because of our being here."

"And at the same time, we can't return to England because we'd be leaving you here to face Rudd alone, with dire consequences, no doubt," Alastair added. "And Melissa can't return without evidence of Rudd's involvement in Jane's death or her boss is going to have her job. Not that that's as important as bringing Jane's killer to justice."

"It's overwhelming, at best," Melissa concurred.

Arran nodded, "I understand all of that, but now that you two do, perhaps you can compose yourselves and we can head inside? I'm not the only one who has to keep a clamp on emotional outbursts, you know?"

Alastair nodded, "Perhaps we'd better discuss what we're going to discuss. Otherwise, I have an odd sense that our conversation is going to sound wooden at best."

"You said earlier, Melissa, that Alastair and you were posing as affianced here on holiday," Arran offered. "Why don't we simply discuss where you intend to visit while you're here, what brought you here, that sort of thing, and then we can make the excuse of going out for a meal to get out of there again."

"Sounds good," Alastair murmured, and they all headed inside.

As if cued by a director, Arran launched into his first inquiry the moment he swung open the door to the apartment, "So, you never mentioned why you decided to vacation in Australia."

"I have family here, and apparently so does Alastair," Melissa replied, then began weaving their tale for their listening audience. "Alastair and I are to be wed within the next month and we wanted to make this a pre-honeymoon, so he could meet this side of my family."

"Why not come after the wedding? An actual honeymoon?" Arran asked.

"Well, if they don't care for Alastair, then the wedding's off, of course," Melissa quipped and Alastair shook his head.

"We both had vacation time available, so we just decided to put the honeymoon ahead of the wedding is all. Her family could never afford a trip to England for the wedding," Alastair jumped in, "and since we needed a place to honeymoon, we decided to kill..." he stumbled over the word and then started coughing loudly, his eyes bulging.

"I'll get water," Arran offered.

"Thank you," Melissa said, patting Alastair on the back. "Choke on your own spit again, darling?"

Alastair glared at her, but nodded, taking the water from Arran and swallowing it in a single gulp, "I do hate it when that happens," he sputtered, settling on the couch. Arran settled onto his lounge chair and Melissa settled next to Alastair.

"Well, I still think it's crazy that we ran into each other. I never knew I even had a brother, until recently. Most certainly never thought we'd meet this soon."

"Me either. So, how did you find out about me? Did your parents tell you?"

"I don't think they knew," Arran replied and Alastair wanted to confirm that. After all, had they known, their reaction to his appearance on their doorstep would have been far different. "I only discovered your existence because I was doing a free month's trial on that genealogy website after my parents told me I was adopted out from England. I never, for the life of me, expected that I'd find family still living; nor that I'd have a twin brother. What about your parents, didn't they ever let on that you had a brother?"

"I was raised in a boy's home."

"No parents?" Arran croaked, unable to hide his shock.

"No parents."

"Is that why you became a priest?"

****

At the mention of the word *priest*, Dunne yanked the headphones off. Suddenly all the information extracted from Jane's investigator was confirmed, which meant that Jane had indeed been in touch with the priest; the twin brother. And that, to him, confirmed their trip could not possibly be as coincidental as that priest attested. His thoughts parroted that of the investigator about what a priest could possibly accomplish. Nothing, as far as he was concerned, but what about the fiancé? Where did she fit into all of this? Was her presence as innocuous as they made it out to be? Did she simply jump a plane with her fiancé because it seemed the right thing to do? He yanked his phone from his pocket and dialed his informant at the police headquarters.

Massey here, came the curt answer.

"It Lachlan Dunne. What did you find out about Melissa Lloyd?"

Oh, um...I'm sorry Mr. Dunne. I was out on an investigation and didn't have time to run the name yet.

"I'll wait then."

Absolutely, Mr. Dunne. Just...shit.

Dunne grinned as he heard a thud, knowing that he was making the Inspector so nervous that he'd dropped his phone.

Sorry, Mr. Dunne. I dropped my phone. Let me just pull up my computer...shit...um...Mr. Dunne, my commanding officer is calling me into his office.

"And...?"

Can you call me back? I'll try to get the information for you as soon as I can, but...well, if he keeps yelling for me and I don't get in there...

"First opportunity..."

I'll run the name, yes sir.

The call disconnected and Lachlan wanted to throw his phone. There was something more going on with this holiday getaway that was going over his head and he hated being ignorant of what was happening. He stayed Rudd's top enforcer because he stayed on top of everything. He wasn't just a babysitting muscle man; he could think and act according to information received, only right now he wasn't receiving the information he needed and it made him angrier than a cat in a standoff with a German Shephard.

He started to dial Rudd and then disconnected the call. He didn't have anything new to impart and he knew Rudd would deny his request to bring Arran and his family in for questioning, even though the urge to stampede the apartment and haul them down to the basement of Rudd Tower was an overwhelming urge. Rudd used certain interrogation techniques when there were sufficient facts to back up use of those techniques; otherwise, as Rudd stated often, he would lose too many good people to rumor. It's why he had men babysit employees long term, to ensure their loyalty. Once ensured, they moved on to other employees or other tasks. It's also why he rarely had to pull out the acid. Fear kept most in line.

Still, something about the couple visiting nagged at the back of Dunne's mind; but he doubted Rudd would take his gut instinct as good enough reason to torture information out of Arran or his visitors. It wouldn't be so annoying if there wasn't a gnawing inside his gut that told him the timing of their visit was far from coincidental. He lifted the headphones and prepared to listen again to their conversation, hoping that they'd slip up and reveal the true purpose of their coming to Australia. All he needed was one thing and then he could put an end to his jumping bean nervousness.

****

"I'm just going to call in and tell my secretary that I plan to take the week off. That way I'm free to play tour guide and to get to know my brother better—and his lovely fiancé, of course. After which we'll head out for dinner at this great little place I know."

Dunne's nerves started jumping again. Arran was taking the week off, which meant he would be gone from ear-shot more often than now; which meant it would be far more difficult to keep tabs on him; which meant gleaning information about his brother's real reason for visiting was going to be downright difficult...unless...

Dunne pulled the headphones off and popped the trunk of his car. He went to the boot and rummaged through all of his gear, grinning widely when he located what he was looking for. He pulled it out of its small housing and then located a tracker also. He laid both aside and pulled out his mobile phone, dialing the number of one of his subordinates. He wasn't going to be able to keep tabs on Arran if they left town, so he was going to have to task out the surveillance to someone else.

"Dunne here," he said as soon as the man answered. "Meet me at Adelaide Terrace. I have a job for you. Be here in ten."

He disconnected, picked up the devices, and trotted across the parking lot to where Melissa's rental was parked. He walked around the vehicle, attempting to locate a placement on the window where it wouldn't be easily visible. Placing a listening device on a car wasn't easy because it either had to be inside or placed on the glass. Since most people locked their doors, placing it inside never panned out, and since it wasn't easy to find a good placement on a window...it's why Dunne used listening devices in or on cars sparingly, but was certainly glad he hadn't discarded his inventory. After all, if Arran were going to be gone frequently or out of town, he needed his associate to be able to continue monitoring their conversation.

CHAPTER TWENTY-FIVE

Melissa stood and walked over to the window while Arran made arrangements to take vacation time. She sighed as she took in the activity along the waterfront in the near distance. She envied Arran this location and wished she were able to live in a place like this, with a view like this.

A movement below caught her attention and she glanced down to see someone trotting across the parking lot. She would have thought nothing of it had the man not stopped and started circling her rental car.

She wanted to start cursing up a blue streak, but with someone potentially listening to their every word, her starting to curse without reason would either arouse suspicion or cause the listeners to believe she suffered from Tourette syndrome. The latter wouldn't be so bad, and it would allow her to relieve her mounting tension, but it would not be a ruse easily maintained. Instead, she fell back on her Buddhist calming techniques, drawing in deep breaths through her nostrils and releasing them slowly.

"What's wrong?" Alastair whispered near her ear. He'd noticed her back go rigid and then the breathing start. He may not know her well, but he did recognize the signs of a near meltdown. Without thinking, he started massaging her neck muscles, until he felt the tension ease. She relaxed into him, allowing his body to hold her upright. After another minute, she moved away and turned to face him, standing as close as was possible to prevent her words carrying. She reached up and pulled his head down, as a lover would searching for a kiss. "Look down at our rental," she whispered close to his ear.

He stood erect to peer over her shoulder, then bent and whispered in her ear, "What am I looking for? I don't see anything."

Melissa spun around and stared at their car. The man had gone, but she knew he'd left them a gift, which meant they would need to take even more precautions, which meant that picking Arran's brain for intelligence was getting trickier by the minute. Rudd was either super suspicious of anything and everything, or he'd somehow discerned her reason for being in Australia. If the former, investigating him was going to be a feat of monumental proportions; if the latter, her life was forfeit. No wonder he'd remained out of prison—he killed anyone remotely threatening. She sighed heavily and turned to lie her head on Alastair's chest. She suddenly wondered where her common sense had been when she'd talked her boss into allowing her to tackle this investigation. If she were on home turf, with her peers to back her up, then this would be a simple matter of acquiring a search warrant for the weapon and arresting Dunne. She wasn't on home turf though, and she had no one to back her up but a former priest and an accountant. She was royally screwed.

"Everything ok?" Arran inquired, then cringed and blushed when he realized how loudly he'd spoken. If their demeanor indicated something untoward as he suspected, they certainly wouldn't be able to answer his query; and if anyone was listening, they'd wonder why that query.

"We were just bemoaning our tiny flat back home," Melissa improvised quickly, moving away from Alastair. "You are fortunate to live in such a beautiful place."

Arran closed his eyes, grateful he hadn't ruined everything. Having to be on guard continually was starting to fray his nerves badly, "I guess I am one fortunate man," he said, trying desperately not to sound sarcastic. "We need to stop by the office to sign off on my vacation request, and then we can head to dinner."

"I thought you were the man in charge," Alastair quipped, as they headed for the door.

"I am, but even the boss has to keep records."

As soon as the apartment door closed behind them, all three sagged against the nearest wall, feeling utterly exhausted.

"I don't know how much longer I can do this," Arran whispered. "It's been only a couple of hours and I'm already drained."

"Me too," Alastair agreed. "All I wanted to do was to fly down here to warn you; maybe to find a way to help you, but we're out of our depth," he concluded, looking at Melissa.

"I agree I allowed my eagerness at catching an international killer and bringing down a mafia boss, to get the better of me," Melissa admitted. "Being here now, I don't know how it would even be possible to get close enough to his henchman to search him for a weapon. Not by legal means anyway. Come on, let's find somewhere more secure to continue this conversation; and just so you know, I'm fairly certain it won't be in our car."

"What did you see, Melissa?" Alastair asked as they headed for the lift.

"I don't know who it was. Could have been just someone looking for valuables, but I am less certain of that than I am that it was Lachlan Dunne, which means that he's likely bugged the car."

Arran sighed heavily, "Is there nowhere we can go without him hounding us?"

Melissa shook her head, "The longer I'm here the more I'm doubtful of that. If we remove the bug, he'll know we're onto him, and grow even more suspicious."

"Let's exchange rental cars," Alastair suggested. "Call in a flat tire or some such."

"That may work. At least we'd have a clean vehicle for a while," Arran readily agreed.

"You don't think he'd be skeptical over the timing?" Melissa asked, skeptical herself.

"Probably, but it wouldn't have any basis," Arran supplied. "Look, Rudd and Dunne are two of the most suspicious men I know. If there were a fly buzzing around their heads, they'd be convinced it was a robot drone. No matter what we do, the red flags are going to keep going up until you find your evidence and arrest them or until Dunne decides we're a danger to Rudd and kills us. Until either happens, we need to be able to talk things through outside of my flat. If we can't do that, I'll go bleedin' mad. We all will."

They all fell silent when they reached the car and Melissa placed a finger over her lips, then began examining the vehicle. She couldn't see anything resembling a listening device, but her instinct told her there was one. She gave each man a look that conveyed to watch what they said until they could get another car, and then they all climbed in.

"Wait, I just thought of something," Melissa said abruptly, climbing back out of the car. Her companions quirked a brow at each other and got out also.

"What's up, Melissa?" Alastair asked.

"I was going to drive, but I think that Arran should. He'd be able to get us where we need to go faster if he didn't need to focus on giving us directions. That okay, Arran?"

"Sure." Arran moved around to the driver's side. Melissa slowly made her way around to the passenger door, inspecting the windows surreptitiously. She'd just about discarded the notion that they'd been bugged, when she spotted a small black speck poking out of the rubber stripping along the rear passenger window. She sighed heavily and then climbed into the car, immediately signaling that they use caution.

"Okay, so we'll exchange the car as soon as we stop by your office then?" Melissa poised as if they were merely confirming a prior conversation.

"We can do it beforehand, if you'd like," Arran replied, "especially if you're certain you're hearing funny noises coming from the engine. I certainly don't want to break down on the motorway."

"If it's on the way to your office, sure."

"Just point me in the right direction and we'll be off." Arran pulled out of the parking lot and headed toward the car rental agency. Dunne's subordinate pulled out his phone and dialed his boss, but the line was busy. He was going to have to let him know of the plans to exchange the rental car and get new instructions; all the while keeping close tabs on Rudd's accountant. If he lost them...he shuddered. He didn't fancy a visit to the basement of Rudd Tower, any more than anyone would.

The three in the car remained silent. They'd spotted the tail quickly, not that Rudd's man went out of his way to remain clandestine. None of Rudd's men ever felt that need as they relied on intimidation to keep people in line. The tension surrounding the bug on the car had them all on edge, and knowing there was someone following them also left each feeling angry, nauseated, and afraid for their lives. Arran forced himself to go just above the speed limit, but his foot wanted to defy his desire to obey the law and slam down on the pedal so to end the tortuous drive and possibly shake the tail. His knuckles were white where he gripped the wheel and when he finally pulled into the car park, he had to work to loosen his arthritic-feeling grasp. All the way into the tiny office, he flexed his fingers in an attempt to work the tension free.

Alastair and Melissa felt no better, each bending their neck and back repeatedly, trying to pop free the kinks that had formed en route.

"How can I assist..." the agent at the counter started, but as soon as he spotted Melissa his face turned ashen.

"Is there something wrong?" She queried, her gaze piercing his in an attempt to read the thoughts hidden behind the giant orbs.

The man quickly lowered his gaze and drew in a deep, nervous breath, "Um...I just...didn't you rent your car for a full ten days?" He asked quickly.

Arran glanced at Melissa who, in turn, glanced at Alastair, as if each were confirming that they all noticed the man's unusually strange behavior. It didn't take a detective to comprehend the cause either.

"My car is making a funny noise," Melissa supplied their cover story. That statement brought to the fore the man's professionalism and his nervous demeanor vanished.

"Well, I certainly am sorry to hear that Ms. Lloyd..."

"You remember my name?" Melissa asked, and the nervous agent returned immediately. *He's behaving as tense as we've felt since our arrival*, she thought.

"Um...well, such a lovely lady and all...quite memorable," he stumbled by way of explanation.

Melissa arched a brow, but forced herself to smile in response to his compliment.

The agent cleared his throat and started checking in the vehicle, "I have one other car available currently," he stated, typing as he spoke. "It a Renault Kangoo. Will that suffice?"

"That will be just fine, I'm sure. Thank you."

The agent continued typing at his keyboard. "The keys to the other rental please."

Melissa laid the keys on the countertop.

The agent slid them aside along with the paperwork for the return. "If you'd sign here, please?"

"What am I signing? I shouldn't need to sign anything to return a rental I've had for less than a day."

"Um...this is stating that you're returning the vehicle because of suspected engine trouble."

"Then you sign it. It's trouble with your vehicle. Not anything that I've caused."

"Um...it's just standard procedure to confirm the renter is returning a vehicle due to..."

Melissa sighed heavily, trying to calm her nerves. She wanted to get out of there fast and this man was hindering that effort. She didn't have a justifiable reason for not wanting to sign his document either, but because she suspected he'd broken the law and turned over her personal information to some dangerous people, she didn't feel like accommodating him further. She also, suddenly, heard a clock ticking in her head. Time was running out to solve Jane's murder and potentially save their own lives.

"Just prepare the rental agreement for the Kangoo, please. We haven't all day to wait."

The agent's skin turned a mottled red, but he quickly printed off the new rental agreement and slid it over for her to sign. She scratched her signature and snatched up the keys to the Kangoo.

"Let's go!"

Arran and Alistair followed her out.

"You thinking what we're thinking?" Alistair asked softly as they walked briskly toward the only other car in the tiny lot. He spotted their tail and nearly tripped over his own feet out of nervousness.

"That he provided Rudd personal information regarding me, you, or both of us? And try not to let on that we've seen our constant companion."

"Yeah, to both," Alastair replied.

"I was thinking along those lines also—that Rudd's men have been here checking out your identities, which means suspicions are raising." Arran reached a hand out for the keys when they reached the car.

"We're drowning faster than we can swim. What are going to do?" Alastair couldn't hide the tremor in his tone.

"The only thing we can do." Melissa didn't elaborate. She just climbed in and waited in thoughtful reserve.

Arran and Alistair eyed each other a moment, then climbed in after her. Each sat in anticipating silence, but Melissa just stared out the front window at the rental building. When she realized they hadn't started moving yet, she looked over at Arran, "Go to your bank first," she said, brooking no argument. Arran nodded and started the vehicle.

"Can I ask what we're going to do?" Alistair inquired, leaning between the two seats. He cared less that they could get pulled over for not having his seat belt buckled.

"We hide," Melissa replied simply.

"Hide?" That hadn't been the response he'd been expecting.

"We're going to do the following as quickly as is humanly possible," Melissa stated, confidence in her rash plan building as she spoke; rather confident that they had no further recourse. "First, we're headed to the bank for you to withdraw every penny you have saved. You do have savings, correct?" Arran could do no more than nod. "Good. We're going to need as much cash as possible. Credit cards can be traced. After that, we're heading to the Passport Office to begin that process. Finally, we're going to pack up what you need for an extended getaway, and we're leaving town for the next several weeks."

"What?" Alistair stated incredulous. "Where..."

"I don't bloody well know! All I know is that it won't take long before Rudd knows that I'm a DS and that we're here for other than the reasons stated. With Rudd's reputation for doing away with liabilities, we'll all be in danger sooner rather than later. The only way I can think of for us to stay alive, is to hide until we can get Arran a passport. Once we obtain that, we'll book a flight back to the UK where, hopefully, we'll be able to put together enough evidence against Dunne and Rudd, with your help, Arran. And we'll be able to bring them down because we'll have Arran as witness to Rudd's illegal activities and Dunne's activities in the employ of Rudd. So, if anyone has a better idea, I'm all ears!"

Alistair flopped back against the seat and groaned heavily. He'd idiotically thought that Melissa and he would swoop into Australia and rescue Arran with little difficulty, and simultaneously locate evidence with which to convict Dunne of first-degree murder. It had been an idealistic dream from which he was now awakening.

"The other option, and one I'm hesitant to put forth, but now that we're on the road in a clean car and my head's swimming is settling a bit; and I'm feeling more rational by the minute..."

"Spit it out, for God's sake, will you? If there's an alternative to run and hide, we need to know what it is." Alastair barked.

"We continue as we are," Melissa replied. "Continue doing what we're doing and the next time Dunne comes 'round, we find a way to relieve him of the knife he carries; which I'll ship to Leeds for testing..."

"We won't live that long, not if they've already discovered who you are," Alastair interrupted. "Even if we can convince them that you're just a DS on holiday here, as suspicious as they are, you know they aren't going to buy the timing."

"I know, but I'm thinking that if we stay, they may try something; attempt to...well, for lack of a more delicate way of putting it...kill us. That seems to be their M.O., right? So, they attempt to kill us and I arrest them..."

Both men burst out laughing simultaneously, but there was no humor in the sound, rather it was a mix of disbelief and derision.

Arran stopped laughing and scoffed, "Do you hear yourself? Do you think they'll set to quaking in their boots if you suddenly whip out your badge and try to haul them in? They'll laugh more than we just did, thrust you into a vat full of acid, and be done with it before you can protest. Same with us all."

"And let's not forget that you don't have jurisdiction here, Melissa, do you? Nor the support of the local law?" Alastair added. "We flew down here on a whim and a prayer in the hopes of somehow relieving a dangerous hitman of his weapon...what were we thinking?"

They pulled into the car park at Arran's bank. When he cut the engine, he turned to face his brother and Melissa, "We run," he offered softly. "Like you said, Melissa. We go from here to the apartment, then straight to the passport agent. We do everything swiftly..."

"And our tail?" Alastair asked brusquely, nodding in the direction of the car that pulled into the car park behind them. "Or have we forgotten that he's following us? He's probably already reported that we've switched cars and are making questionable stops. We won't make it out of town. And then there's the viability of lying low this long, if we're even able to outmaneuver the hooligan following us. I don't know about you guys, but I'm nearing broke. And you, Melissa, how long did your boss give you to solve this? I'm sure that you're not on an endless stipend. Do you think that if you call your superintendent, he'll approve an extended stay where you're just hiding out? Not likely. More likely, he'll demand you return posthaste. Then there's the cost of changing our flights. I understand that we need to stay, because we can't leave Arran alone here to face Rudd, but I'm having a hard time wrapping my head around how we're going to accomplish this. And did anyone think about how we'll retrieve that passport if it's mailed to Arran's apartment? We already know someone's constantly on watch..."

"We get it. We've got our work cut out for us, and that's if we even manage to stay alive long enough to get our plans started. The best thing we can do is to take it one step at a time," Arran interjected. "I'll go clear out my accounts. Don't worry about money. I have more than enough to see to our expenses if we decide hiding is the best option. I even have a place we can go, too, which won't cost us anything. Let me take care of closing my accounts, and then we'll discuss it further en route to my apartment to pack out of there."

Without awaiting a response, Arran climbed out of the car and walked into the bank, leaving Alastair and Melissa alone to stew over what next reasonable steps they could take.

"What are we going to do, Melissa?" Alastair whispered. "I've never been so unnerved, so out of my depth...and before you say it, I know I brute-forced my way into this. I could've left well enough alone. I just never anticipated that it was going to be this ..." he let the sentence hang, could do no more than lower his head, shaking in uncertainty. "What are we going to do?" He murmured again after a moment.

"We're going to lie low," Melissa whispered, placing a hand on his lowered head. "Then we're going to get out of Australia. I don't have a doubt that Rudd will send Dunne after us, and when he does, I will have jurisdiction and the backing of the Leeds police department; and we will see justice done for Jane."

"You sound so certain of yourself," Alastair replied, his worried gaze boring into her confident one, but her confidence was all for show.

"I've never been so frightened in all of my life," she admitted, and laid her forehead on his shoulder. "Like you, I think I bit off more than I could swallow. I wasn't thinking about the ramifications of flying halfway around the world without any backup; I wasn't thinking of anything other than there was a single thread attached to a giant quilt, and I figured that if I followed it, pulling along the way, the whole thing would magically unravel. It's not the rationale of a detective sergeant, it's the impetuousness of a juvenile. People watch a cop show on the tele and assume that everything goes smoothly until the bad guy is taken into custody, but life doesn't work that way. What was I trying to prove?"

"That you're capable and professional, and worthy of your rank. Maybe without realizing it, you're searching for validation."

"I don't know. Maybe. I may be uncertain as to what I was thinking, but I do know what I'm thinking now."

"And what would that be, DS Lloyd?"

Arran climbed back into the vehicle, just as Melissa was set to explain. "If we're going to lie low for a while, we aren't going to do so without being productive. Let's get the passport application and packing underway, but first—how's your ability to outwit the witless, Arran?"

"Pardon?" Arran asked, starting the car and heading for the passport office.

"I want to ensure we're at least alive to forward my plans, so I need to know if you're capable of losing Rudd's man following us."

Arran took the exit to his apartment, "Let me pack first, because we won't get another chance. We shake this guy, there'll just be another..."

"...waiting at the apartment," Melissa completed with a sigh. "This is so convoluted."

"That's because we're trying to plan, run, and hide simultaneously," Arran supplied.

"I don't think we'll be able to think straight and relax until we're certain we're safe to do so," Alastair added.

"And we won't know that until we're packed out of your place," Melissa furthered. "If that tail has already managed to report the exchange of our rental vehicle, it may send up enough flares that we'll have a welcoming party waiting on us when we arrive."

"If you still hold any priestly powers, Alastair," Arran quipped without humor, "I'd suggest you use them now, because we'll find out in a few minutes whether we have an unfriendly receiving committee at my place."

Alastair crossed himself as they turned into the car park.

CHAPTER TWENTY-SIX

This is Dunne. What are you reporting?

"Arran Masters and company exchanged the rental car they had, so I won't be able to keep tabs on them outside of their apartment, other than tail them..."

Where are they now? Dunne snapped, concerned that his bugs had been discovered.

"They just pulled back into Masters' apartment complex."

Dunne signed audibly, taking that as a sign that all was still well, but why switch vehicles?

Call the rental agency and get an update on why they exchanged vehicles. If I don't answer when you call back, just leave a message and let me know what the agent has to say.

"Will do."

Dunne disconnected and immediately dialed his police informant's direct line. The rental car exchange could be an innocent act or it could be bad news. He needed to get on top of things now, and that meant getting answers to questions still hanging. One of which was the identity of Arran's visitors.

Massey here, the cop answered with a confidence that quickly faded when he heard the reply.

"Lachlan Dunne. What information have you for me?"

Um...I just got back to my desk. What was the name of the...

"Melissa Lloyd from Leeds, England," Dunne snapped.

Right. One minute and I'll just punch that in. Um...okay...results coming in now. There are five Melissa Lloyds in the Leeds metropolitan area.

"Five?"

That's right...um...one is a head mistress, one works with the Leeds police, one is...

"Stop! Did you say Leeds police?"

Yes, she's a Detective Sergeant...

"Photo available?"

Easy enough to obtain. The Inspector replied, swallowing hard.

"Good! I'll be there in half hour. Have it ready for me."

I'll meet you in the car park in half hour.

The call disconnected and the gears in Dunne's head started turning rapidly. The pieces of the puzzle were starting to fit and it was forming a disturbing picture. First, the reporter digs up information on a priest, Arran's brother, then that reporter flies to England to meet with that priest; now the priest shows up in Australia with a woman, potentially a Detective Sergeant with the Leeds police; but to what end? That's where the puzzle got confused and unclear, the pieces missing. Surely, if she was a DS, she'd know that her powers in Australia would be nonexistent; that she wouldn't be able to arrest anyone without assistance from the local...he picked up his phone and dialed Massey again.

Massey, the inspector answered.

"If that woman is a DS from Leeds," Lachlan started without preamble, "wouldn't she need to stop in at the station to seek assistance or even just as a courtesy?"

If she were investigating anything she would, but I can tell you now that I've not seen nor heard about any visiting officers.

That brought Lachlan a modicum of relief, but not enough to where all doubts subsided, "Did you find a picture?"

I did, yes. Lovely thing.

"Describe her to me," Dunne ordered.

Aren't you just going to pick it up?

"No, just describe her to me," Dunne repeated more firmly.

The detective had never been more relieved to follow one of Dunne's dictates. He couldn't fathom Dunne showing up at the station and he being directly associated. It wouldn't bode well for his career, unless every cop were as dirty as he was, which he couldn't risk testing; not with a wife and three children.

He pulled up the image on the computer, *Okay, I have a woman in her late thirties to early forties. In this photo, she's got shoulder-length brown hair. Eye-color is hard to distinguish, but it looks as if they are brown. That the woman you're searching for?*

Dunne breathed deeply through his nostrils. The provided description could match any woman, but it also matched the priest's fiancé, "Put me through to your supervisor, now!"

I'll need to put you on hold for a minute.

"Just get me through to him."

Massey learned long ago not to ask why when dealing with Dunne or any of Rudd's goons, but he sincerely wanted to right now. Had he done something to upset Dunne so that he was about to be reprimanded or fired? As he listened to the call forward sound ding in his ear, his nerves began jumping faster and faster as his mind rewound the few conversations he'd had with Dunne over the last few hours. He'd been responsive to his every whim, even though he'd not necessarily been able to jump through the hoops when immediately placed in front of him. He swallowed hard, fear elevating when his supervisor didn't answer. Would Dunne request his presence at Rudd Tower if he wasn't able to produce his supervisor? He was just beginning to formulate reasons for keeping his job when his supervisor picked up.

This is Turner.

"Massey, sir. I have Lachlan Dunne on line 3 for you, sir."

There was silence for a minute, which Massey readily understood. No one really wanted to get a call from Dunne; no one who knew the man, that was. The line went dead and Massey stopped breathing. Surely his supervisor wasn't deliberately shunning...he glanced down at line 3 and noticed the light was no longer blinking. Massey released his breath in a loud whoosh. He was both relieved that the call had been picked up and nervous also. Were they discussing him? Number 3 light went out and his extension rang. He knew he was about to find out whether he still had a job.

"Massey here."

Come see me.

The line disconnected again and Massey stood. His legs were like jelly and his knees knocked as he strolled across the room to his supervisor's office. He rapped quickly.

Come in!

"You wanted to see me, sir?"

"Have a seat," Turner replied.

Massey quickly complied, sitting rigid in front of his boss.

"Seems you and I have a common acquaintance," Turner stated in a tone dripping with disdain.

Massey closed his eyes, waiting tensely.

"For years I thought I was the only one," Turner continued, his tone taking on a sad relief. "And since we don't know how many of my constables are on Rudd's payroll, and can't assume everyone is, we need to approach this wisely."

"Sir?"

"We've been instructed to assist in delivering..." Turner paused, looking down at the notes he'd written, "Melissa Lloyd of the Leeds Police, her fiancé, whom I take it is a priest from England; and that priest's brother, who just happens to work for Amherst Rudd, to Rudd Tower. Right now, Dunne has a man following the trio; however, to ensure cooperation, Dunne felt it was best to have a police presence. That presence will be you. So take yourself over to this address," Turner continued, tearing a strip off his notepad and passing it to Massey. "You'll meet up with one of Dunne's men, and from there you'll escort the three to meet with Rudd."

"Yes, sir." Massey stood to leave. He felt there should be more said, but in his heart preferred nothing else be said. The fewer words spoken, the better. He was relieved that he wasn't the only cop forced to be crooked, and was even more relieved that the other person on Rudd's payroll was his boss. That meant his job would remain secure for as long as he stayed on Rudd's good side. As he left his supervisor's office, he heard the shredder and grinned. His boss was getting rid of his written notes. Always wise.

He grabbed his gear from beside his desk and headed toward his vehicle. He didn't know what these three had done to piss Rudd off, but he knew that whatever it was couldn't be good—not if Rudd was seeking an audience with them. He'd heard rumors about people being summoned to Rudd Tower and never leaving. What happened to those people he didn't know, and didn't want to know. It was just his goal never to be one of those people.

As he pulled into the car park of Adelaide Terrace, he immediately spotted Dunne's associate. It wasn't hard to miss any of Rudd's goons because they all looked alike—walking pit bulls in suits. He pulled his patrol car alongside the man's Hyundai i30 and lowered his window, "Dunne sent me."

"They went into the building about ten minutes ago. We'll wait here and then take them into custody when they come out."

Massey mentally shook his head. This thug was speaking as if they actually had a legal right to detain these people and take them to see a mafia boss; spoke as if he were a police constable and legally allowed to arrest anyone he so chose.

"Dunne tell you what law they are meant to have broken so I can make it sound on the level?" Massey tried to keep the sarcasm out of his tone, but knew he failed.

The man arched a brow at him, "You're the cop, you think of something."

Massey's eyes widened and his brain shut down. How in Hell was he supposed to think of something? He didn't even know these people, had no knowledge of their activities—legal or illegal. He sighed loudly, then started going through the statutes in his head. He needed something that he could spout to be official sounding, so they wouldn't have cause to question his detaining them. Of course, he could just make something up too, but that was a risk should it backfire. The only thing that popped into his head was the code against unlawful assembly. It was a stretch to think that these three individuals were conspiring to disturb the peace, but at least if he were questioned at any point in future, he would have a legitimate response rather than 'because I was ordered to'.

****

"You're tense again," Alastair whispered into Melissa's ear causing her to jump. She glanced at him briefly over her shoulder and then turned again and pointed out the window to the car park.

Alastair moved around her and looked down in the direction she was pointing. He looked at her and was about to comment when she placed a finger against her lips and shook her head.

"I'm packed for our getaway," Arran said, carrying a large suitcase from the bedroom.

"What took you so long? We finished packing ages ago," Melissa quipped, but pointed to the front door. Both men knew that meant they needed privacy to talk and headed into the hallway.

"I can't help it if I'm a picky packer," Arran bantered, walking toward the front door. He pulled open the door as quietly as possible, and all three stepped outside. Just as quietly, he pulled the door closed.

"I saw a police constable with Rudd's man," Alastair stated immediately. "Think he'll chase him off? Give us time to get out of here unnoticed?"

"Police constable?" Arran queried.

"Yeah, Melissa spotted one conversing with Rudd's man."

"If we have an opportunity to leave, we should grab our luggage..."

Melissa placed a hand on Arran's arm, stalling his departure. She shook her head and frowned, "I watched them for a while. That constable has been chatting cordially with Rudd's man for the past ten minutes. He isn't there to warn him off about loitering. That could only mean one thing."

"Your identity has been found out and they are using local law enforcement to escort you to Rudd," Alastair concluded. "Probably all of us."

"We're not going to be able to get a passport or be able to flee and lie low, are we?" Arran asked.

Melissa shook her head, "And we can't head back inside to discuss strategy either, because your place is bugged; and we can't get out front to the car park and drive off because we'll be waylaid the moment we step foot outside."

"What are we going to do now?" Alastair asked, trying to keep the alarm out of his tone.

"Is there a back door out of this place?" Melissa asked Arran.

Arran nodded, "But we'd still not be able to get to the car without being seen."

"We wouldn't, no," Melissa agreed, "however, you two should be able to with the right diversion."

"I don't follow," Alastair interjected.

"This is the only thing I can think of to ensure Rudd and Dunne get what they deserve; and whether you two like it or not, I need your acquiescence, otherwise we may as well save Rudd the effort and kill ourselves now."

"I don't like the sounds of where this is headed," Alastair murmured.

"I'm not overly fond of the direction either, but it's the only recourse now," Melissa asserted.

"Let's hear it," Arran replied with a heavy sigh.

"Okay, first things first—while we can, pull out your mobile, Arran," Melissa instructed.

CHAPTER TWENTY-SEVEN

Alastair and Arran stood along the side of the building, nerves jumping as they waited for the opportunity to sneak to the rental car and leave. Fortunately, it was a busy time of day, as workers were returning home and then leaving soon after to go socialize with friends. It was fortuitous timing because it meant that their leaving would be unlikely noticed. All they needed...

"There she is," Arran whispered hoarsely, peering around the side of the building.

"They've spotted her," Alastair whispered, anxiety lacing his words, as he nestled up beside Arran and peeked around also.

"Their backs are to us. We need to go now," Arran whispered harshly, grabbing his suitcase and moving rapidly across the car park.

Alastair picked up his and Melissa's suitcases and followed along behind, praying with each step that Melissa would hold the attention of the constable and Rudd's henchman long enough for them to leave.

He hated her plan, but she'd made a valid argument and had given them no room to quarrel; had all but told them what was going to happen and brooked no dispute. They'd finally conceded because she was the officer and they were simply a priest and an accountant. They had no experience in dealing with this sort of horridness.

They reached the rental, grateful it was not within line of sight of their adversaries. With little pause, they yanked open the rear doors and tossed in their baggage, shutting the doors with contrary force from how they'd opened them. Equally cautious, they climbed into the vehicle.

"Why aren't we going?" Alastair asked, frantic when Arran just sat there, counter to their critical need to escape.

"There's a couple of people headed to their own cars. I want to use their departure to mask ours."

"And hope that Melissa can find a way to break free and join us?" Alastair asked hopefully, watching the three individuals in front of the building engaged in apparent heated exchange. It had seemed such a long time since they'd set their plan into motion, but it had been less than half hour, all totaled. Even less since Melissa exited the building and been immediately confronted by the two men in Rudd's employ.

"If she can convince them that we're in for the night, they may leave her be…"

"Then shouldn't we wait a few minutes longer? See if she goes back inside? If she does, she may sneak out back and join us…"

"Even if she manages to sway them into leaving, their attention would be no longer diverted. It would be a matter of minutes before we're spotted. We haven't long to wait, but while we do, why don't you get online and locate the information we need to get the video into the hands of those it needs to be in, and keep praying that Melissa's plan proves successful."

Alastair sighed heavily and thought tacitly that he'd sighed in one emotional state or another more in the last week than at any other time in his life. That made him sigh again while he punched up his search engine and started combing for the information they needed to put an end to this ugly mess once and for all. "If this is likely to bring down Rudd, why didn't we think to do it before?" Alastair muttered.

"Because before, Melissa was acting like a cop and concerned with simply finding evidence; before we were concerned with being able to talk without being spied on; before we were simply trying to ensure we stayed alive; before our focus was trying to get me out of the country…take your pick. In any case, we thought getting to freedom was paramount, and it kind of still is; but at least now, we have ammunition." Arran heard the first engine roar to life, "Time to go," he said, turning over the ignition.

Alastair felt a tear break free and trickle down the side of his face, then closed his eyes in supplication that nothing untoward befall this woman, who'd gone to such lengths to reunite him with his brother, and—if her plan succeeded—to save their lives, "Do you think we'll survive this?"

Arran nodded, his lips sealed in a tight frown as he waited tensely at the head of the car park, waiting his turn to merge into oncoming traffic, "I think we might."

"And Melissa?"

For that query, Arran had no response. He hit the accelerator at the first opening in traffic and headed toward the coast.

CHAPTER TWENTY-EIGHT

"What criminal code was that again? After all, if you're going to place me in a squad car, I'd like to know precisely what it is I've done to warrant it; especially since we've only been here on vacation a very short while. Not exactly time to plan a major heist or some such."

Melissa was livid. She knew that she'd needed to divert the attention of these men, but she could hardly believe her ears when the constable cited some law that she was in violation of and requested that she accompany him. At the same time, she was relieved that it gave her something to argue over, giving Arran and Alastair the time needed to leave the area.

"I'm taking you in for questioning under criminal code II, Chapter IX, Section 62(1)," the constable repeated, his skin turning a deep red beneath his collar.

"So you've said; however, you still haven't relayed what that code is precisely," Melissa pressed.

"I'm not at liberty to divulge that information. I've simply been instructed to bring you, and your two mates, in for questioning, which I intend to do," the officer stated more firmly, "so, if you'll precede me into the building, we'll go and escort those gentlemen down."

"They aren't in. They left some time ago to run errands," Melissa stated smugly. "Since I wanted to do something else, I told them I'd meet up with them later for dinner..."

"You're lying," Rudd's henchman interrupted, walking up next to the police officer.

"And you are?" Melissa queried, knowing full well who he was.

"Get her to the car. I'll go check out the apartment," the man ordered the officer, ignoring Melissa's query, then turned and headed inside.

"My supervisor's an asshole too," Melissa said to the officer as he escorted her to his car.

"He's not my supervisor," the officer muttered, obviously embarrassed at being so harshly commanded to do something.

"Ah...well, no matter." She knew he wasn't the supervisor, but she needed to maintain a ruse of ignorance. What she really wanted to do was whip out her credentials and demand he treat her with the respect she deserved as a fellow officer. "I really wish you would explain to me what crime my friends and I are supposed to have committed," she tried again, partly to stall and partly because her nerves were on fire. She knew when she agreed to act as a diversion that there'd be a chance her life would be at risk, but another part of her hoped they'd just question her and let her return to the flat. After her brief encounter with Rudd's thug, she was more convinced her life was in danger. Years of service as an officer of the law had honed her senses and they were shouting at her that she wouldn't survive this encounter if they managed to get her into that police vehicle.

However, the officer declined to engage with her further. He opened the door and started to guide her in, but she stalled again, "If I'm going to be sitting here waiting, do you think I could go in and use the restroom first?"

The officer closed his eyes in agitation, but nodded, "Make it quick. My instructions are to take you and your friends in for questioning."

"So I gathered, although I can't fathom what questions we could answer," she reiterated, then headed toward the building. She expected him to follow her in, but he just leaned against the car and crossed his arms. Apparently, he wasn't worried over her attempting anything—not with him outside, and Rudd's henchman upstairs. She knew that it wouldn't be long before he returned downstairs, which left her precious little time to plan an escape.

Melissa headed to the rear exit debating with herself the wisdom, knowing she wouldn't get far on foot. She only prayed that she'd get far enough to catch a cab before they noticed she was missing. She ducked out of the rear door and shimmied over the fence along the property line, then slid down the steep embankment to the edge of the slough. Without slowing her pace, she took off running along the edge of the marshy ridge, determined to put as much distance between her and death as possible.

CHAPTER TWENTY-NINE

"We're here, so what do we do now?" Alastair asked, scanning the ships docked around the harbor.

"We do what Melissa suggested and hope it's even doable," Arran replied, fear and exasperation lacing his tone. "Okay, where to start?" He murmured rhetorically.

He and Alastair stood rooted, glancing about in uncertainty, when a security guard approached, "Help you mates?"

"We're seeking passage to Europe. Was hoping someone could point us in the direction we need to go," Alastair said in a rush.

"Got a passport, there's not a reason why you can't just go commercial," the security guard replied, eyeing them with suspicion.

"My brother has one, but I don't; and it'll take three to six weeks to procure one, as you're probably aware," Arran stated honestly, but then his candor derailed and he started manufacturing details. "Plus, my brother's a priest, so we don't have much in the way of funds for commercial travel. A friend told us we could book passage on a freighter far cheaper; and since we've just been informed that our mother is ill…"

"I see," the guard interjected thoughtfully, but those two words screamed disbelief, and for a brief span, both brothers felt they'd made a serious error in judgement; but then the guard spoke up again, with a shrug of his shoulders, "Not really my business why you need to take a slow boat to China, as it were. Most of the captains, moored about a mile down, will provide a berth for those willing to pay."

Both men drew in a deep breath simultaneously, "Appreciate your assistance," Alastair replied, then both men turned and climbed back into their car. "I can't believe it may be as easy as that."

"Nothing easy about this. We're looking at a minimum month's journey, if we're fortunate enough to even book passage on a freighter."

"At least we'll be out of reach of Rudd's clutches. You'll be safe," Alastair rejoined.

"Yeah, but we won't know the outcome of anything…potentially ever!" Arran retorted, then continued with anger lacing each word. "We're sailing blind into the unknown. We won't know if we'll reach land, at all. Freighters sink, you know? We won't know if Rudd will have Dunne in England waiting for our arrival. We won't know if our message is received and if anything is being done about it. Neither of us are employed as of this moment; and, to top it all off, we won't know Melissa's fate for over a month either. Dear sweet Jesus, we're mad for even attempting this!"

Alastair sat silently for a few minutes contemplating his brother's outburst, and then finally replied quietly, "You know, I don't have a lot of faith these days. Too many things have happened recently that's had me questioning…well, everything; but one thing I do have faith in is this plan. Maybe not faith, but belief that's it's our only way to stay alive. Yeah, boats sink, but not that often, surely. Yeah, Dunne may be awaiting our arrival in England, but after a week or so, he'll likely conclude we never returned to England, because he won't know we've even left Australia. We can't toss away our only opportunity of survival because we're unemployed now or sailing into the unknown. We have to be stronger than that—for Melissa's sake—and we have to believe, more than anything, that'll she'll be on the next flight possible, and will be the one waiting on our return."

Arran nodded, "All the emails sent?"

"I meant to tell you that the video file is too big. I kept getting an error stating that I can't upload a file bigger than 25 Gigabytes? I have the email addresses, but…well, quite frankly I'm not technologically savvy enough to know…"

"Hand me my phone back," Arran interrupted, extending his hand. "I'm glad I asked before booking passage on a freighter, because it isn't likely we'll have WiFi on the ship. There's a couple of options available for sending large data files. Hopefully, our recipients have access to one of them."

"It was smart of Melissa to have us record our statements, in the event something happens to any of us. Maybe, with my eyewitness testimony, and all that you and she witnessed, someone, somewhere, will be able to finally hold Rudd and Dunne accountable."

"I'll add a note explaining where we are and when we're estimated to arrive…"

"I wouldn't do that—at least not to all of the recipients," Alastair interjected.

Arran quirked a brow, awaiting an explanation.

"We're sending this, not only to Melissa's superiors, but to Perth's Commissioner of Police, the Governor of Western Australia, and to Jane's editor at the paper…"

"And we don't know who we can trust not to be in Rudd's pocket," Arran finished.

Alastair nodded, "I'd say that we should only inform Melissa's superior, and also tell him that we fear she could be in grave danger. Maybe he'll send backup to help her or to ensure she gets home safely."

"Good idea," Arran said. He selected the video file, then hit the share icon. "First, I'll create a link, so I can email the file also. Redundancy is never a bad thing, especially in this circumstance." He copied the link, and set about emailing all of their intended recipients, ensuring that only the police in England knew their whereabouts, their intentions, and their intended arrival date on England's shores. He then selected the file again, clicked share, and searched for Drive. "Crap! I don't have access to Drive on my phone…wait, I'll download it. Then we'll have sent the file a few different ways." He sighed when he completed his task, then turned off his phone to conserve his battery, tucked it in his pocket, and sighed heavily again, "Well, I guess it's time to see if we're able to get off this rock," he started the car and drove the mile down the coast to where the freighters were moored.

Once parked, Alastair stepped from the vehicle. He went to retrieve their luggage, but Arran told him to wait, "No need to haul those around while we search for passage."

"Good point. Well, let's do this!"

CHAPTER THIRTY

Melissa continued her speedy pace for more than fifteen minutes. When she was confident that she wasn't being followed, she began the ascent up the embankment and then climbed the fence, coming out behind a convenience store. She sat down on the curb and pulled out her phone. Now that she knew she wasn't going to be able to meet up with Alastair and Arran, she needed to put the next part of her plan into motion.

First things first was to call Arran, to confirm he and Alastair were safe. She dialed the number, but it went straight to voicemail. She closed her eyes against the mounting frustration and tried once more. Straight to voicemail.

"Arran, it's Melissa. Just checking in to see how you and Alastair are getting on. Give me a ring when you get the chance. If all goes well, we'll meet up soon. Godspeed." Melissa disconnected that call and then rang up the car rental agency.

Budget Car rentals. How may I assist you today?

"This is Melissa Lloyd. I rented a car..."

I remember Miss Lloyd. What can I do for you?

"I need to report the car was stolen."

Stolen!

"That's correct. This morning, from the Adelaide Apartments car park."

I'll send the police around to complete a report.

Melissa was ready for that response, "I'm afraid I won't be available to fill in a report. My flight leaves in half hour. I had to take a cab to the airport. I just wanted you to know so that you wouldn't charge me for any further use of the car. You have my address on file, so if there are any documents you need me to sign, simply mail them to me and I'll return them posthaste."

But I have you for a two-week rental…

"That's correct, but an emergency back home is cutting my vacation short. I intended to return the car this morning, but…well, as I've stated, it was stolen. I'm nearly to the airport."

I apologize for any inconvenience this may have caused you.

"Hopefully, the police will locate the vehicle undamaged. I need to run. Thank you for your help."

Melissa disconnected the call and looked at her mobile with a smug grin, "Report *that* to Lachlan Dunne." She'd lied about nearly being at the airport, but she was gambling on Dunne not sending an army after her, if he thought she was safely off the island.

****

The agent did indeed dial Dunne the moment the call with Melissa disconnected.

Melissa Lloyd called. Reported her rental car as stolen.

Dunne hung up on the agent without responding. He was livid. Not only had the officer, and his subordinate, failed to bring the three to him as instructed, but now all three were in the wind, apparently had dumped the vehicle also, so there was no way in which to trace their whereabouts; *and* his subordinate hadn't called to let him know of this development. He would deal with that after he updated his boss. He dialed Rudd.

"Dunne here. We've lost them."

Explain.

Dunne launched into a brief update and then waited. He knew he was now at risk for a visit to the basement at Rudd Tower, and that *would* be his next stop if he couldn't provide Rudd a solution, which he requested immediately.

What's being done?

"I've contacted all officers on our payroll with names and descriptions, and I've also ensured that the airport is sufficiently covered so that none of them get on a plane back to England, since one of them reported that's where they were headed." He hadn't as yet done any of those things, and if the agent's accounting was correct, he may have already missed the opportunity to reacquire them; however, he wasn't about to tell Rudd that.

I want them found and brought to me...

"Give me twenty-four hours."

The call disconnected, which meant that Dunne was now on the clock. He immediately dialed the man he'd had at Adelaide Apartments. The man picked up the phone on the first ring.

"I've just been made aware of the debacle, but what I'd like to know is why it wasn't you that made me aware."

Officer Massey and I set out immediately after her...

"Her? Not all three? Where are the brothers?" Dunne asked harshly.

She came out alone. I went up to the flat to get the brothers, but they weren't there. She'd said they went out alone earlier to run errands, but I never saw them leave. When I went up to search, I left her with Massey, but she gave him the slip. Since she's on foot, there's only two directions she could've gone initially, so Massey and I are on her heels. She won't get far. I'll ring you as soon as we've located her.

"She called the rental car agency. Said her destination was the airport; said her flight was scheduled to leave..."

Not on no international flight, she isn't, the thug interrupted. *Has to be at the airport two hours ahead of a flight, and I was chasing her not half hour ago.*

"So it was a ruse," Dunne sighed, relieved. "Collect Officer Massey and get there now. You'll not find her on foot. If she gets the opportunity, she'll call a cab company and be at the airport fast. If she books a flight *at* the airport, she can potentially leave soon. We can't let that happen."

What about her mates?

"I'll send another officer to the apartments to watch for them."

Why do you think they split up?

"I don't know," Dunne snapped and abruptly ended the call. He immediately placed a call to the police department and requested the superior officer. His heart was pounding in his ears while he waited for the call to be connected. In all the years he'd worked for Rudd, never once had things gone this far awry. He didn't like it. He was used to being in control and controlling anyone he needed to also. Yet within the space of a few days, Arran Masters, his twin brother, and a DS from Leeds were yanking control from beneath him. It made his blood pressure raise dangerously high.

Turner here.

"Lachlan Dunne. We have a major problem."

What can I do to assist? The query was offered in a tense tone, the displeasure at having to ask evident. Dunne cared less.

"I need a couple of officers over at Adelaide Apartments to keep a look out for a set of identical twin males, and as many men as you can send to the airport to keep an eye out for a DS from Leeds. The twin brothers may be at the airport also."

I don't want to sound disagreeable, but without photographs…

"You'll find DS Lloyd's photograph if you do a search of police officers in Leeds, England."

Leeds?

"That's right. You've had a DS on Aussie soil for the better part of a day, investigating Amherst Rudd and me, and you did nothing to prevent it."

I didn't even know she was here, and why would a DS from England be investigating your boss?

"Our boss, and don't you be forgetting that again. As to the whys, that isn't your concern, *mate*. Finding her is. Now get her picture printed and distributed. As for the twins, I have a picture of one of them. I'll text it to you. Since they look alike, it'll suffice for both. You get it to your officers. That should be sufficient to ensuring we round those three up soon." He heard Turner sigh on the other end, and surmised he wasn't one-hundred percent on board, but they never were. Those who did Rudd's bidding only did so under duress, but if that kept *him* alive, he'd pressure the Governor into helping in the search. He had a mere twenty-four hours in which to produce those three, and at this point, he didn't much care if it was done so in body bags. "Are my instructions in any way unclear?"

I'll look for your text.

"Good. The next thing you can do is call the cab company. See if any cabs picked up a single female fare headed to the airport. Also, isn't there a way to track someone via their credit card purchases?"

That would take a warrant. Got a judge in your pocket?

Dunne gritted his teeth, "I don't need a judge, because the three we're looking for aren't being arrested, so find a way to get me the information. I need to locate them!"

Understood.

As soon as he finished up that business, he got into his car and headed to the airport. There were only so many flights in and out of Perth headed to London, and he intended to have every single one of them watched; every cab arriving also.

CHAPTER THIRTY-ONE

Melissa's next call was to a cab company. While she waited, she went into the convenience store to purchase sunglasses and a ball cap. She was going to make damn certain that no one could easily identify her.

After her purchases were completed, she paced the sidewalk out front, waiting on the cab to arrive, her nerves jumping every time a police car drove by…and there appeared too many of them.

By the time the cab arrived, fifteen minutes later, she was fairly crawling out of her skin, and had chewed a few of her nails to the nub.

"Airport?" The driver asked as soon as she climbed in.

"Rapidly yes." Melissa sat back and closed her eyes. Despite repeated breaths, slowly in and out, she couldn't calm herself. Alastair, Arran, and she had been in deep, shark-infested waters from the moment she'd convinced her boss she could only make an arrest if permitted to fly to the land down under. Now, all three of them were on the run, trying with desperate urgency to get off the island before being apprehended, and potentially tortured to death.

There was no doubt that Rudd would not allow them to live—not at this juncture. If he didn't feel they'd become a threat, he wouldn't have sent his henchman to the apartment complex to bring them in for a chat. And she knew that the only chat Rudd intended to have with the three of them was to discern if they'd passed any information on to anyone else prior to…she shuddered.

Never, in her time as an officer of the law, had she felt so completely incompetent and out of her depth. Once more, she began to question why she thought it had been a good idea to come here in the first place. Did she really think herself capable of finding evidence against a mob boss and his henchmen on foreign soil? Was she just concerned that Alastair would be flying into a fiery pot of boiling water if she hadn't accompanied him? Did she somehow feel responsible for him because he'd been traumatized—first by the death of his brother's fiancé inside the church confessional; and second by the revelation of an identical twin brother for whom he'd had no prior knowledge…until the fiancé turned up in his confessional.

Had she done her job properly at the onset, she never would have need to worry over Alastair, because she'd have thrown his ass in a jail cell and done her investigation from the security of her cubicle, using the telephone. She sighed loudly and opened her eyes.

They were approaching the departure terminals of the airport. Melissa sighed again…this time in relief. All she needed to do was to find a flight out of Australia, and at this point, she didn't much care as to the destination. If she had to hop over to New Zealand first, she'd do it. Her only concern was getting away from Lachlan Dunne.

Her relief was short-lived when she glanced out the window. There were police swarming everywhere, and even if she wasn't the target, it was a bigger bet that she was.

"Don't stop," she told the driver, who'd just pulled curbside.

She saw him knit his brow in confusion, but since his meter was still running, he didn't argue. He glanced over his shoulder and carefully merged back into oncoming traffic, "Where to now?"

"How far is the nearest seaport?" Melissa asked.

"About a forty-five minute drive," the driver responded, and then pulled back curbside.

The hairs on Melissa's arms stood erect as police walked about, scanning their phones and then the faces of people walking by. She no longer doubted she was the person of interest. "Why did you pull back over?" She queried, trying to keep her tone level.

"Since you wish for me to turn the vehicle in the opposite direction for an even lengthier jaunt, I need to ensure I am going to get paid; that you aren't just using my cab for a joy ride."

Melissa sighed in relief, but was still aggravated that her trip was stalled. She looked at the meter. It read fifty dollars. A quick calculation of the return trip, would mean another hundred or more, easily. Add to that the cost of her passage…she did a quick mental calculation of the cash given her by Arran. If she spent too much on cab fare, she'd be stretching her ability to pay for a way off Australian soil, especially since they all agreed to avoid use of credit cards. She pulled her wallet out and paid the fifty dollar fare.

"Is there a bus terminal nearby?" She asked. It may take her five times longer to get to her destination riding the bus, but it would also cost far less than taking the cab; and while she was eager to get out of Australia, she was equally eager to stay out of Rudd's clutches. As with all of her actions of late, she began to question the wisdom of taunting the rental agent into telling Dunne her destination was the airport. She'd only done so because she felt confident that she could get there and catch a flight before anyone showed up to stop her. It had been yet another error in judgement, but she'd wanted to draw any searches away from Arran and Alastair. Keep the hounds on her heels.

"At the end of the curb, there's a ticketing booth. Should be able to procure passage there," the driver said, interrupting her musings.

Melissa's nerves started jumping again. Getting out of the cab and walking the length of the terminal meant passing a dozen or more officers on high alert. "Can you drive me down there?"

"Cabs aren't permitted in that area. Sorry."

Shit! Okay, just get out and keep your head down. She thought to herself; however, as soon as she stepped from the cab, she knew she stood out as one of the very few who didn't have luggage. She drew in a deep breath, and started walking, praying that she wouldn't resemble the photo the officers were scanning on their mobiles. As she strolled along the walkway, trying to appear as casual as possible, she was grateful for the foresight to purchase sunglasses and a ball cap, for the few officers she'd passed thus far merely glanced her way, then moved their gazes to other people. *I may not be the target after all,* she mused hopeful. The bus terminal came into view, about a hundred feet down the walkway, and she wanted to pick up her pace, but knew it wouldn't be wise to draw undue attention. It took an immense effort not to break into a run.

She was becoming surer that she wasn't the target as she passed more officers who gave her no more than a fleeting look, thus began to relax.

When she reached her destination, she took her place in the queue and waited patiently for the next attendant to free up so she could purchase her ticket. There were no buses parked curbside, so it could be an even longer wait before she could leave this area, but as long as she kept her head down and drew no attention to herself, she was confident she could evade capture.

As the minutes ticked away, her nerves began to bounce again. There were far more people awaiting a ticketing agent than she liked, so she scanned around quickly to see if there were a kiosk nearby, and then wished she'd just kept her head down. Four officers were walking determinedly toward the queue. As casually as she was able, she glanced about at the other people nearby to see if any registered alarm at the presence of so many officers, but most displayed no more than a passing curiosity. The sureness she'd gained that she wouldn't be spotted in her disguise fled and she began questioning her next move.

The decision came quickly, when she glanced briefly at the approaching officers and knew they were looking directly at her. If she remained where she was, she could simply try to brush off any likeness to their photo as being her doppelgänger, feign ignorance; but just as quickly dismissed that as she didn't have fake identification to back it up. Without hesitating further, she decided her best bet was to get lost, so she stepped from the queue, moving at a fast clip toward the nearest door to the airport terminal. She didn't know precisely where she was going, or how she was going to extricate herself from this particular predicament, but she did know she needed to hide in order to formulate a plan. She was confronted with a serious quandary now, and no longer felt an assurance that she would find a way to elude police custody, much less find a way to leave Australia.

CHAPTER THIRTY-TWO

We've caught sight of a potential suspect. Any constables in the vicinity of terminal one, she's ducked inside. We're in pursuit. Last seen, she was wearing a ball cap and shades, jeans…

Dunne listened to the report come in over the radio he'd been provided by a constable upon arrival at the airport. He immediately headed in the direction of terminal one, his gaze scanning people that passed. As soon as the report finished, he pressed the talk button, "There's a chance that she ducked into a restroom, or place of business, so do not simply look out for people dashing along the terminal. And don't forget to station officers at the terminal exits; and ensure those officers check the identity of all women departing alone. Now that she's in the terminal, we want to make certain that she remains here until we locate her."

Melissa did in fact duck into a restroom, but not one designated for female use. Instead, she veered off from the women's restroom and went straight into the one designated for men. She ignored the questioning looks of the few men standing at the urinals and deposited herself inside one of the two available stalls. She slid the latch locked, placed a seat protector, and sat down. Uncertainty squeezed at her insides like a corset and she had difficulty drawing breath. She was in a world of trouble and had no plan on how to get herself out of it.

If she left the restroom now, it was a strong likelihood that she'd be apprehended sooner than she could swap out her disguise, but she knew that it was futile to remain ensconced where she was. Not only would someone need use of the stall before long, but one of the men she encountered may very well decide to send a security officer to check on why she'd hidden herself away in the men's restroom.

No sooner had that thought registered than a voice interrupted her musings.

"Ma'am, are you okay?"

Oh no! Her mind railed and panic started to set in. *It could just be a concerned citizen,* she thought, trying to calm herself, but if she responded then she'd be required to leave the bathroom. She drew in a deep breath and held it, hoping that her silence would encourage his departure. It didn't.

"Ma'am, I need to know if you're okay. I'm not certain you're aware or not, but you've come into the wrong bathroom. If someone is harassing you, you need to let me know, so I can escort you somewhere that you'd feel safe. Either way, I can't permit you to remain here, so please come on out."

Melissa felt trapped, but she knew she'd not be able to stall further. When she slid the latch aside, she closed her eyes in supplication that it would be an innocuous security guard and not one of the officers that was on the search for her.

She slowly pulled the door open and affected an embarrassed look as soon as the security logo on the shirt caught her eye, "I am so sorry," she murmured, "I just had to go so badly that I didn't look at the signage closely enough."

"I quite understand, but you need to use caution in future. Women aren't the only ones who dislike having their privacy intruded upon by the opposite sex," the guard reprimanded.

"I'll not let it happen again," Melissa replied in an appropriately apologetic tone, nodded, then headed toward the door, her stomach a knotted mess. A quick glance in either direction was devoid of uniforms, so she made a mad dash down the passageway, her gaze scanning for any place useful to purchase anonymity. If she were hungry or in need of reading material, there certainly were plenty of opportunities afforded for those; however, locating a place to buy any type of clothing was scarce. Near the end of the strip, she spotted *Rip Curl* and immediately headed inside. Ordinarily, she'd have little use for flip flops, board shorts, or other sunny sundries, but right now wasn't ordinary. She was bordering desperate.

She pulled a pair of board shorts and a hooded crop top from a nearby rack and made her way to the register. She nearly choked at the amount rung up, but could ill afford to be fussy over price gouging, when her life was at stake. She swiped the bag from the counter top and headed back to the restrooms, this time ensuring she ducked into the correct one.

Her hands were shaking as she shed her clothes and donned the new ones. She then took the clothes she'd been wearing and shoved them in the bin, along with the ball cap and sunglasses. She stood, staring at her image in the mirror for the longest time, then turned on the faucet. Ducking her head over the sink, she started splashing water in her hair until it was nearly saturated. She flipped it back, then fingered it, until it was slicked down and tucked behind her ears.

It wasn't the best disguise, but the officers would be searching for a woman in jeans, ball cap, and sunglasses; and if they had an image of her, it most likely came from her personnel photo from several years prior. Looking at the woman in the mirror, she knew that she only resembled her younger version if her hair was coiffed and her makeup done. Without the accoutrements, she could easily pass for a different woman. She was counting on the officers not glancing too closely at the resemblance, merely giving her a quick once-over and then letting her pass.

Squaring her shoulders, so that she wouldn't appear a nervous female on the run, she walked from the women's bathroom and headed for the nearest exit. She'd still need to go back to the bus stop to acquire a ticket, but again, she hoped that her attire would mean being overlooked by those in search of her.

She spotted an older woman, rolling two suitcases awkwardly along and sprinted over.

"Why don't you let me take those for you," she offered.

"Oh, I'm fine," the woman replied and kept walking.

"Are you certain?" Melissa persisted. "I don't have any luggage, so my hands are free. At least let me take one for you. My father would be sorely displeased if I didn't. He raised me to be respectful, especially when in a good position to aid someone in need."

"Oh, all right," the woman conceded after looking Melissa over cautiously. Fortunately, no red flags appeared to go up, which surprised Melissa, as she now looked like an aging rock star ready to tackle some waves. Melissa wasn't going to question her luck, however, and took one of the bags, following alongside the elderly woman.

"So, are you just visiting, like me?" Melissa asked. The appearance of casual conversation was important if she were to waltz right by the officers at the door.

"My daughter and son-in-law live here," the woman replied. "I'm coming to stay with them for a while. They're going to sponsor me, since I'm too old to work any longer."

"That's very lovely of them."

"Well, I'm not so certain at the moment, since they aren't here to greet me," she replied sardonically. "What about you, dear? You're British from the sounds of it, so why are you here? And without luggage?"

"Oh, I'm visiting family also," Melissa lied, "and I'd have luggage, if it hadn't been lost."

"Oh my! That does seem to happen all too often nowadays, which is why I try to only carry that which will fit in their overhead bins. Since I'm moving though, I had to pack quite a bit more," she laughed, nodding towards her burdensome luggage. "I do hope yours gets returned to you soon."

"Me too," Melissa smiled, "especially since I don't want to wear this get up for too long, nor do I want to spend my entire vacation funds on new clothes."

The door was drawing nearer, and the officers had yet to glance suspiciously in her direction. Her breathing was beginning to return to normal.

"Grandmother?"

Melissa jumped at the piercing yell so close behind her, that she nearly dropped the handle to the suitcase.

"Samantha, dearest!" The elder woman exclaimed, turning toward the young girl dashing toward them. "My family is here," she told Melissa, leaning down to scoop her grandchild in a giant hug.

Melissa closed her eyes in frustration, but pasted on a smile when the daughter gave her a look, brow furrowed in question.

"I was just assisting your mother with her luggage," Melissa stated, passing the handle over to the daughter. "But now that you all have arrived, I'll just be on my way." Melissa placed a hand on the older woman's arm, "Enjoy your new life," she murmured.

"Thank you for the help," the woman replied, then Melissa was forgotten, as the family reunion continued.

This close to the door, Melissa didn't stand a chance of finding another traveler with whom to latch onto, and to make matters more nerve-wracking, the commotion caused by the family had drawn the officers' attention.

Smiles flitted across the officers' faces as they watched the interaction between granddaughter and grandmother, but then they were looking straight at her. One of the officers looked and then looked away, but the other looked at her, glanced at his mobile then looked back. She wanted to turn away, but didn't want to incur suspicion, so she started walking toward the adjacent doors.

Just behave as if you have nothing to hide and that you are just arriving, she thought; however, a movement in her periphery told her the game was up, and she'd been discovered. She drew in a deep breath of resolve, knowing that her only chance now was to make a run for it and jump into a cab before she was waylaid.

She took off at a run, pushing open the door to the terminal with enormous force; but never expected it to fight back. In fact, it seemed to argue that it would not be rushed open; that it would take its own sweet time. She realized that it was a hydraulic-driven door, meant to open and close slowly to prevent injury. Without realizing it, she'd chosen to exit through a portal for the physically challenged. The door finally opened sufficiently for her to squeeze through, and then she bolted down the sidewalk towards the cab stand.

She wanted to glance back over her shoulder, but didn't dare risk it. Just as she was nearing the first cab in line, a man stepped from beside a beam and stuck his foot out, tripping her. She stumbled and then went skidding along the pavement, grunting as her head collided with the concrete surface.

Blackness threatened to descend, and she willed her mind to stay alert. Then she saw the smirking face of Lachlan Dunne bending over her, "Someone wants a word with you."

Her phone chose that moment to ring, and she was in no position to prevent Dunne from jamming his hand into her pocket to retrieve it. He answered it, but didn't speak; not until the person on the other end paused, "We've got your friend, and make no mistake—we'll find you and your brother too."

CHAPTER THIRTY-THREE

"I wish we'd have thought this out better," Alastair complained. "We're in no position…"

"We discussed this, Alastair," Arran interrupted. "You and I both know we don't have a choice in the matter."

"Yeah, we do. We go to the police. Not all of them are on Rudd's payroll, surely!"

"Yeah, and you know which aren't? Perhaps the ones who are will be kind enough to wear a badge stating *on Rudd's payroll.*"

"And you and I both know that Melissa is going to be spitting mad when she finds out we didn't catch that boat…"

"She'll understand. There's no way she wasn't standing there when Dunne answered the phone. It was *her* phone, for God's sake, and if I hadn't decided to check for messages before the boat set off…well, we know that we'd have never known her fate. Now, at least, we have a chance to do something."

"We *were* doing something. We were getting out of Australia. She was counting on us to get to safety…"

"We got the information safely out there, and that's going to be our bargaining chip with Rudd. When he finds out that we've notified every official we all know…"

"He's going to take it as a bluff and kill us where we stand!" He fell quiet, staring out the window at the passing trees, as Arran raced away from the docks, heading straight back to downtown Perth. When Dunne had answered his call to Melissa, he was certain that she'd be taken to Rudd Tower, and that terrified him.

Arran was deep in thought also. He shuddered at the thought of another woman dying at the hands of one of Rudd's thugs—all because he decided he didn't want to play by their rules; all because he decided that he wanted no part of an illegal enterprise. Now he'd convinced Alastair, the brother he just found, that they two were her only chance for getting her out of Rudd Tower alive. The only issue he was having currently were details on just how they were going to execute that plan—in fact, he hadn't provided Alastair a single detail on how precisely they were supposed to get to the basement of Rudd Tower and out again, with all of their extremities intact. He knew his brother was placing a lot of trust on his shoulders, and it was weighing heavily on him.

Alastair finally broke their drawn-out silence, whispering fearfully, "I hope, for all of our sakes, that you know Rudd's weaknesses, because we're relying on you at this point."

Arran shook his head in dejection, "I know all of them, but it does me no good beyond having shared that information with Melissa's superiors and Jane's editor at the newspaper, but since we haven't received word from either of them as to what is going to be done with that information…we go in there and hope that we can negotiate for her release. And if he thinks it's a bluff, we show him the video and the sent receipts. That should convince him that his dirty laundry has been aired and that his empire is on a crumbling foundation."

Alastair sat looking at his brother for a short while, trying to decide if *he* really believed their chances of survival were truly that good. He determined that his brother was all bluster, running strictly on adrenaline and some sense of honor.

"I have a suggestion," Alastair said quietly, as a thought struck him based on something Arran had said.

"We're not going to the police," Arran retorted.

"No, not the police."

CHAPTER THIRTY-FOUR

"She spoke very highly of you, sir," Arran said respectfully. They were seated across the table from an older man at a pub around the corner from the man's office, but Arran wasn't all that convinced that Alastair's plan would prove fruitful. Still, it was better than his own plan, which was to rush Rudd Tower and take Melissa back with fists flying. For them both, this was a last ditch attempt at gaining leverage against Rudd, when there didn't seem there was leverage to be had. "Is there anything that you know…"

"I know she's likely dead," Oliver Carter murmured sadly, taking a giant gulp of his lager. After a quick breath, he downed the remainder and then signaled for the server to bring another, "just like Jane died, and my other star reporter before her, and Jane's investigator. People that cross Amherst Rudd don't live to tell the tale. That's why I insisted we come here to talk, because I don't know if Rudd's bothering to bug my offices again, since Jane is no longer…sorry," he muttered, then drew in a shaky breath before continuing. "I brought these things with me, because I wanted you to know what you're up against, as if you, Arran, don't know that firsthand already," he finished, sliding the jewel-sized box containing Arran's fingernails across the table. "This was the warning sent to Jane when she started sniffing around too much; and this," he slid the other box across the table, "was the warning sent to me the first time I sent my prior star reporter sniffing around Rudd's businesses. I keep them as a reminder that crossing Rudd is a certain death sentence. And if you think that DS Lloyd is still alive, when Rudd knows she's here investigating…"

"We have to assume she is," Alastair interrupted, "until we know she isn't. And if we are working together…"

"Who, precisely, is *we*?" Oliver interjected sharply.

Arran and Alastair looked at each other for a moment, then Alastair nodded slightly, indicating that Arran explain.

Arran drew in a deep breath and started, "Rudd has stayed in power because he keeps individuals in line by bullying them, threatening them; killing off their loved ones…" He stopped for a moment as that last statement slammed into his gut like a sledgehammer. He leaned over the table and closed his eyes against the pain swirling in his chest and belly. Alastair placed a hand in comfort on his shoulder, and Arran sat up. He smiled weakly at his twin brother, drew in another deep, steadying breath and continued. "We've already set Rudd on his toes, or he wouldn't be hunting us down. That means we've made him nervous, so apparently he isn't used to being challenged by more than one person simultaneously. Too many witnesses to dispose of at once, something's bound to go wrong. So, we've determined to get as many people as are willing to go up against Rudd in a very public way. He can't…he won't…be able to silence us all. It's time he knows his threats no longer hold water."

"And you think us three can make that impact?" Oliver asked incredulous.

"I made a phone call to a few other people," Arran stated. "They're en route as we speak. Those who can, who are willing, will be here within the hour; or late tonight, into early morning."

"And while we're waiting on them," Oliver interjected, "DS Lloyd is likely being…"

"We know," Alastair interrupted, not wanting to hear how their delays could spell disaster for Melissa; how she was possibly being subjected to unbearable torture, as they sat drinking their lager. It made him ill in his stomach. "But we have to do this now, while Rudd is vulnerable. We have to do this now, so that no one else gets killed."

"And where do I fit into this scheme of yours?"

"While we're waiting on the others to arrive, you and I," Arran said, suddenly feeling hope return, "are going to have a nice chat for your morning edition."

"But before that, we need to procure a few rooms at an obscure motel somewhere for everyone arriving."

"Just precisely how large is this army of yours?"

"We'll fill you in on the way," Arran said, plunking the money on the table for the lager. The three men stood and headed out of the pub; the twins feeling better about things than since the whole calamity began. It was short-lived.

Arran's phone rang. The caller ID information had his steps faltering. He showed it to the other two men, "It's Amherst Rudd."

"You may as well answer it," Oliver offered. "If we're going to set things in motion, we're going to have to start that snowball rolling sometime."

Arran answered the phone, "Is Melissa still alive?" He asked immediately.

Ah now, Arran, you should know better than to think I'd harm anyone. I just want you to come in so that we can talk and straighten out this misunderstanding.

"I just need to know…"

And I don't discuss business over the phone, Arran. I'm not a fool, so don't mistake me for one. You're my accountant. I simply need for you to come in, so we can discuss business.

"I'm on vacation, remember?" Arran stalled, waving his hands at Oliver and Alastair, who just stood eyeing him worriedly. Finally, Arran pushed the mute button, "Ideas on what to tell him to stall coming in so that we can finalize our plans? Ideas that aren't going to get Melissa killed immediately?"

"Tell him that you're out of town, since you already mentioned being on vacation. Tell him you'll be back in the morning, and will come then," Alastair offered. Arran nodded. He punched the mute button again and waited for Rudd to finish talking about the 'business' discussion they needed to have as soon as was possible.

"I'll be back tomorrow morning. I'll come in around nine a.m."

Then I'll expect you back to work at nine sharp.

The call disconnected and Arran tucked the phone back into his coat pocket, "I don't think he's done away with Melissa yet. I think he's using her as a guarantee to get me back there. It's me he wants to silence."

"Let's go get checked in somewhere, and let everyone know where we're meeting up. We need to make certain we get our ducks in a row fast, so we aren't swimming about scatterbrained on this." Oliver shook his head.

"What's wrong?" Arran asked.

"Oh, I just realized my wording wasn't very good. Ducks in a row make for easier targets."

Alastair laughed without humor, "Yeah, I suppose they do, but our group of ducks are quacking mad, so we won't be going down that easily."

CHAPTER THIRTY-FIVE

It was two-thirty a.m., and Oliver, Arran, and Alastair were sitting at the table going over the details of what all they were going to include in the news story. They had until four a.m. in which to finalize the details, and for Oliver to write out the exposé that he planned to run in the six a.m. edition of the newspaper. So, as tired as they all were, they knew it wasn't time for any of them to sleep.

It was that sleepiness that had Alastair a little snippy, and he asked why they had to review the video again, when they'd already sent it off to Oliver. Oliver abashedly admitted to deleting their damning email before reading over all of the information because he was afraid of becoming Rudd's next victim. When Alastair asked him what changed his mind about it all, Oliver stated, "There really is power in numbers. It never dawned on me that any of us stood a chance against Rudd, but we were going at him one at a time."

So, they wearily started reliving it all again. They got to the part of the video where Alastair was explaining his experience with Jane's death. Oliver looked up from his note-taking and sighed, "I can't use Jane's murder in the story, or my suspicions on my other reporter, or that of Jane's investigator."

"Why not?" Arran asked agitated.

"Because it's hearsay. There's no evidence that Rudd or Dunne was involved. I could face jail time if I print something like that without evidence to back it up."

They all fell silent and then Alastair spoke up, "You write the piece, not as an exposé—because even with the information provided, there still isn't any evidence to back any of it up, as you say. It's just our word against Rudd and his army of attorneys. So, we write it as a general...what do you call a newspaper piece where people are just providing their accounts or stories or opinions?"

"An op-ed," Oliver supplied.

"A what?" Arran asked.

"An opinion editorial. An op-ed. That's those pieces in newspapers that you read that are written by people, not necessarily affiliated with the newspaper, offering their opinions. Sometimes they're highly inflammatory, but since they're opinions, they aren't necessarily legally libelous. That would be perfect for what we're trying to accomplish. We three will simply offer eyewitness accounting of what we've personally experienced, without naming names. I'll let you two write your accounting out, and I'll write about the packages received as a warning. That is evidence that cannot be overlooked; and since none of us will mention Rudd's name or any of his associates, we'll be covered," Oliver continued, his excitement rising. "Be certain that you don't mention him in your accounts. Keep it generic. Understood?" Both men nodded. "And Alastair that was great thinking."

An hour later, the three men finished up, and Oliver collected their pieces, "I'll trust that you two kept to the parameters I specified, because I haven't time to edit them before getting them to press. I'm heading there now. Send up a prayer that I'm not prevented…"

"We aren't going to think that way," Arran interjected. "As far as Rudd is aware, your involvement in any of this vanished with Jane's demise. He hasn't any reason to suspect that you're working with us."

"Let's hope so. Why don't you two try to get some sleep, like your Mom and Dad next door," Oliver suggested, then shook his head, "You know, when you told me that it wasn't going to be just us three storming Rudd Tower, I thought you'd found an army, but instead your elderly parents show up at our door. What are we supposed to do with that?"

Arran laughed shortly, "Oh, they're just here to bear witness. I don't know for certain, but I'm kind of hoping that Rudd won't go after the old—not without giving it a second thought, at least. I certainly never intended they be in harm's way."

"Besides, we have an ace up our sleeve—we hope," Alastair concluded.

Oliver nodded, and slid on his coat, "I'm still waiting on you to share just what that ace is."

Just then a knock sounded on the door. The three men looked at each other, caution in the gazes. Arran carefully stepped over to the door and peered through the peephole. There was a badge being held up by a man on the other side.

"The police," he whispered.

"How did they find us?" Oliver asked, his tone anxious. "We didn't inform any of the local…"

"It's got to be someone from Melissa's unit. We called them in, remember?" Alastair offered, and everyone breathed an audible sigh of relief. "Of course, I was hoping they'd send more than just one man, so it may not be them. So, let's err on the side of caution," he murmured and walked up to the door. "Who's there?" He called.

"Chief Inspector Wright. Leeds Police." He called back.

"Shit!" Arran exclaimed, releasing the chain and pulling the door open. "We never expected Melissa's superior officer to make the trip down, sir. We don't know how to thank you for coming."

"You can start by letting me in, and explaining what in Hell is going on," Wright snapped, pushing past Arran.

"I'll head on to the newspaper. Get things rolling on my end," Oliver stated, heading out the door, then turn and smiled, "Nice ace."

CHAPTER THIRTY-SIX

"Melissa dropped off the face of the map, and then I get an email with some disturbing video; and then that's followed up by a phone call from one of you telling me that my officer has been abducted by the man she was here investigating," Wright ranted. "Just what is going on here?"

"I was going to offer coffee," Arran murmured, "but he's running full tilt already."

"Have a seat, sir," Alastair offered. "We'll fill you in."

"The video filled me in," Wright snapped. "Right now, I need to know why I'm here, and just what we're planning to do to get Melissa out of that acid-wielding madman's clutches."

"At least *he* watched the video," Arran said sarcastically.

"Yes, I did. I had heard that Amherst Rudd was bad news; and I can't say I was thinking straight sending Melissa down here alone to try to find the evidence needed to bring him down. I guess the thought of nailing a big fish like Rudd to the wall got the better of me. Now, instead of evidence, we've got serious trouble."

"We've got a plan," Alastair offered.

"Which obviously doesn't include the help from local law enforcement. All of them bad then?"

"We don't know, but since we don't know, we can't rely on any of them."

"I don't have jurisdiction…"

"We know, but if we can get probable cause, you may be able to sway the powers that be to shut Rudd down," Arran stated, confidently.

"And you have a way of getting that probable cause?" Wright asked, doubt lacing his tone.

Arran nodded, "We think so, yes."

"And if this is so doable, why didn't you two—and DS Lloyd—not think to do it before this volcano of a mess erupted?"

Arran and Alastair looked at each other, then Alastair sighed, "In all honesty, I think we three were still reeling from events…"

"Events?" Wright interrupted.

"Jane's death, meeting my twin brother, trying to stay one step ahead of Rudd's thugs...basically trying to stay alive. We were desperately attempting to find somewhere out of earshot of Rudd and Dunne in order to make any plans at all, but his men were on us at every turn. It got to the point where we felt the only reasonable avenue was to get out of Australia as fast as we could. That seemed the only way we were going to be safe enough to plan anything..."

"Then Melissa got snatched," Arran continued the explanation, "which got Alastair and me off of Rudd's radar long enough to duck out of sight. We've used that time to plan; something we'd been unable to do until now."

"And what is this grand scheme of yours that's going to save Melissa's skin and nail that big fish to the wall?"

"We're going to tell you all about it," Alastair offered.

CHAPTER THIRTY-SEVEN

"I'm really not certain I like this idea at all, Arran," Barbara Masters said worriedly over their morning breakfast. They'd all met up outside of their motel at 6:30 the following morning, and headed over to the breakfast nook, an amenity of their motel chain. None of the men were particularly hungry, but Barbara Masters was a force to be reckoned with, and she insisted they all have a nourishing repast before heading off to face danger.

"I know, Mom," Arran replied, then took a sip of coffee, "but we've discussed this. CI Wright made a good argument against all of us storming Rudd Tower. Greater numbers seemed a good idea when we were planning it all out, but he's right that we wouldn't be doing any good…"

"Other than freeing Melissa," Alastair interjected. "That will definitely be a positive to all of this."

"Right, but it wouldn't do anything towards toppling Rudd's empire; and after all we've suffered through, there needs to be some favorable outcome," Arran concluded.

"And since it is Arran that Rudd is expecting…" Wright added, but Arran finished.

"Then it's me that needs to be the one going in there alone."

"Yes, but that's my problem with all of this," Barbara persisted. "You both stated that Rudd was intimidated by larger numbers; that he wouldn't be worried over taking out a single person…"

"And we still believe that," Arran interjected. "I will be going in alone, but I won't be alone, will I, Chief Inspector Wright?"

"Not if we can acquire what we need before your nine a.m. imposed deadline; so can one of you that's finished eating get on your phone and see about locating the place we need? If they don't have that here, then we're going to be going back to the twin's plan of storming the building; and I have a feeling that won't bode well for any of us." Wright got up and went back over to the breakfast bar to refill his plate with eggs and bacon, while Arran's dad, Tim, and

Alastair began the search for a place that would help them with their revised plans.

"There's The Spy Store," Tim piped up, "but it's about twenty minutes away, in Welshpool. If Arran is going to get back to Rudd Tower by nine a.m., we're going to need to head that direction now."

"Are they open?" Arran asked, quickly downing the remainder of his coffee.

"I can't find that information on their website, so they'd better be," Tim answered.

Without hesitation or further discussion, everyone filed out of the breakfast nook en masse.

"I'd tell you two to stay here," CI Wright said, walking up next to the Masters, "however, it's probably better if we all stay together. That way, when the time is right, we'll be ready. *Are* you both ready for this?" He asked, concern not only about allowing civilians near a police operation, but also that they were retired and on the elderly side.

"My boy needs me, sir," Tim answered. "Hellfire couldn't keep me back."

CI Wright nodded, "Okay, so climb in with me then. I have more room in my rental."

The two vehicles peeled out of the motel parking lot, their driving imitating their urgency—both in getting what they needed quickly, but also in their elevated hope that CI Wright's plan might just save their lives.

CHAPTER THIRTY-EIGHT

Melissa sat, unwillingly strapped to the metal chair, agony wracking every inch of her body. She wished she'd devised a plan of escape in the event she was apprehended, but she'd been too busy trying to evade capture since her arrival; and now it was too late.

"At least Arran and Alastair won't get caught up in this," she murmured to herself. That thought pushed some of the pain away and she breathed a sigh of relief. That relief was short-lived as Lachlan Dunne came strolling into the room.

"Mr. Rudd sends his apologies. He thought he was going to be coming down to speak with you himself, but his plans changed, so, you only have me to answer to—quite literally. The more you withhold the answers to my very simple questions, the worse off you're going to fare; and before you come back with the old cliché of "you're just going to kill me anyway, so why should I answer any of your questions" bullshit, know this—my methods will ensure you're around for a very long time, suffering intense agony, and you may never die from it. So, let's start with the one main question that Mr. Rudd wants to know the answer to—what information did you, and the brothers, pass on and to whom?"

Melissa remained stoic, not even bothering to look up at Dunne, who huffed in frustration. He reached for the vial on the table next to her, but she refused to flinch.

Her feet already bore several holes, burned through with the acid he was using to elicit responses, which made her wonder how she was keeping her mouth shut in the face of such ruthless torture. It wasn't as if she'd gone through a special training which would prepare her for such brutality. In fact, she *believed* that he would stop her anguish if she would just answer his questions.

That was another thing that made her wonder about her current state of mind—what was her silence truly gaining? His knowing the answers to questions posed wasn't going to change anything. The information was out there already; the damage done—hopefully. And then it struck her—she still had people to protect. Those who knew

Rudd's dirty secrets would be next in line for this chair if she revealed to whom she sent the information.

Another thought nearly made her smile—she was just too damned stubborn to give in. Her daddy used to tease her that the more someone pushed at her, the more obstinate she became. It was true. She hated being bossed about or bullied, and tended to shut off and close up—tighter than a clamshell.

"Well, we'll keep working on loosening up that tongue of yours," Dunne murmured, as a drop of acid splashed on the back of her hand. It loosened up her tongue quickly, for she began screaming in renewed agony. When she quieted, he asked the same question again. She tightened her lips and clenched her jaw. He held the dropper over the other hand and let the drops impale it, quickly eating at the flesh. She screamed again, and then passed out.

Dunne sat the vial down and went back to the only other piece of furnishing in the room—a metal cabinet. He opened it and pulled out a different vial, then carried it over. He pulled out the cork stopper and waved it beneath her nose. Melissa jerked several times, then her eyes fluttered open.

"Okay," he said, then put the smelling salts on the table next to the vial of acid, "let's continue, shall we?" He murmured, asking the question again. When there was no response, he squeezed the dropper top and grinned as acid began gnawing a hole in the top of her thigh, like a ravenous leviathan.

CHAPTER THIRTY-NINE

It was eight-forty-five when the two vehicles pulled into the back lot of Rudd Tower. Before departing the car, Arran rolled the window down and scanned every pole nearby to ensure this part of the lot wasn't being monitored on camera. They needed privacy, and the element of surprise. When he was certain they were out of reach of any electronic surveillance, he put the car in park and stepped out.

CI Wright and his parents met up with him and Alastair, and they immediately set to work.

"We're running short of time," CI Wright complained, "so we aren't going to have a test run beforehand. That, I don't much like."

He was busily prepping the items they'd purchased, grateful he'd had Tim drive, while he started the setup and pairing with his mobile while en route from Welshpool. Had he waited, ignoring his instincts, they would never have been ready before the imposed nine a.m. deadline. As it were, he needed only to position each item in a discreet location.

"Why do I need two again?" Arran asked, already nervous over the prospect of having just one discovered.

"Redundancy saves lives. Besides, we'll quite literally get them coming and going," Wright quipped, "and remember, the minute that I record anything at all even remotely incriminating, the four of us will enter and save the day."

"I know I said that it was better to wait to attack collectively, in the hopes that Rudd would think twice about retaliating, but I'm not so sure now…"

"This isn't the time for second guesses, son," Tim interrupted. "Not when the life of DS Lloyd is at stake—yours too."

"Okay, Dad. You're right, and since the early edition of the paper went out three hours ago, it won't take long before someone in Rudd's organization gets wind of it and a bullseye gets planted on Oliver Carter's back. That, we need to prevent."

"And getting killed ourselves," Alastair added.

"Okay, both apps are up and running, simultaneously," Wright stated. "You get going. We'll be ready at a moment's notice."

Arran gave a quick glance at his watch—eight-fifty-five. He closed his eyes, drew in a deep breath then moved to his car. "Oh, Alastair," he called, pulling his mobile from his pocket. "Keep it, in case you need to call in more backup."

"What backup would I call in?"

"I don't know. Maybe dial the local police. If not all are in Rudd's pocket, maybe someone will come to our rescue, if pressed. Don't chance that though, unless it looks as if our merry group of bandits are done for."

Alastair nodded and grinned thinly, without humor.

"Be seeing you soon. I hope." Arran quipped and then climbed back into his car and drove to the front of the car park.

CHAPTER FORTY

Melissa knew that Dunne had been correct in his assertion that he could torture her, nearly endlessly, and she'd not die—although she did pass out repeatedly. Still, death avoided reaching its bony hand out for her and pulling her into oblivion. Her mind cursed death for ignoring her; for allowing her to suffer heinously at the hands of this psychopath.

At this point, her mind taunted her far more than Dunne tortured her, for it incessantly pointed out that even if she did manage to somehow free herself from the bindings that held her securely to the chair, her body was riddled with holes. And if she didn't finally succumb to shock-induced death, infection would likely set in, potentially killing her even more slowly and painfully than the acid. Basically, her mind told her it wasn't hopeful of surviving this encounter.

Still she sat mute, determined to protect anyone else involved in this, with her last breath. That determined, continual silence, was finally wearing on Dunne's nerves, and he'd taken to pouring larger amounts of acid on her legs and arms—simply as a method to vent his frustrations. He'd never had acid torture fail in gleaning the information he sought for his boss. Generally, one drop was all it took to persuade his victim to spill their guts.

To him, having this woman sit here and defy logic was maddening. Added to the chaos his world had become since she and that priest arrived from England, and he was fairly foaming at the mouth with rabid anger.

One of Rudd's other thugs arrived, just as he was about to pour a dollop of acid on one of Melissa's breasts, and he grinned wickedly—a quiet promise that he'd be doing just that as soon as he attended to the interruption.

Melissa's head fell forward and she passed out yet again.

"Okay, I'm coming. Rudd knows he's here, right?"

"Yeah, he told me to tell you to bring him down here, and he'd be along momentarily to tend to him personally."

"What about her?" Dunne asked, tilting his head toward Melissa.

"Boss said we don't need her anymore, but to hold off finishing her in case leverage is needed against the accountant."

"Got it," Dunne said, then followed Rudd's other enforcer from the room, and boarded the elevator.

Death chose that moment to make its appearance.

CHAPTER FORTY-ONE

"Hello, mate, where are you headed?" Lachlan greeted—a little too amiably.

"Mr. Rudd called me back into work early; ended up having to cancel my vacation," Arran replied, desperately attempting to maintain his composure; to feign ignorance of everything.

"And what of your mates? Where are they?"

As if you didn't know, you bastard! He thought crossly, but to Dunne, he replied, improvising, "My brother is staying at the beach house. There wasn't any reason for him to come back with me and have his vacation shortened also. Melissa…" he stopped. He couldn't finish the sentence, because they both knew where Melissa was at that moment—and it wasn't on vacation. "Well, if you'll excuse me, I believe that Mr. Rudd was expecting me in his office at nine sharp."

"Mr. Rudd is detained, and asked that we meet him downstairs," Dunne stated, and Arran couldn't help but notice it was done so in near-glee, and that set Arran's nerves to jumping—that, and the mention of downstairs. However, anger quickly replaced his fear when he noticed Dunne's ridiculous grin.

He's enjoying this too much.

And Dunne was. He'd nearly lost control of the situation during the past couple of days; had felt his sense of domination slipping; however, since he'd seized DS Lloyd and had the accountant waltz back into his domain, he started to feel in control again, which was fueling his body with euphoria. The only one left to apprehend was the priest, and he knew that he could do that blindfolded. *Ah, it feels good to be cock of the roost again*, he thought.

"Why does Mr. Rudd need to meet with me downstairs? If he's detained, I'll just wait for him in my office," Arran interrupted Dunne's musings. He was stalling because he didn't fancy returning to that abhorrent room of torment in the basement. He didn't want to see Melissa being subjected to acid—if she were still there; didn't want to be the one strapped in the chair.

"Sorry, mate, but we have our instructions. Downstairs we go, if you please." Dunne moved aside and motioned toward Rudd's dedicated elevator.

Arran hesitated, glancing toward the front doors. He wanted to run again, wanted to forget all about this plan and go catch that boat—sail around the world for as long as it took for Rudd to forget his existence.

But then he'd go after everyone else—dad, mom, Alastair; and he'll likely be after Oliver Carter before this day is over. You've come this far because you want to put an end to the fear and death, and because you need to try to free Melissa. She put her life at risk for me—for all of us. The least you can do is to be brave.

His mental speech completed, Arran sucked in a deep breath and headed for the designated elevator. Thus far, he'd captured not nary an incriminating word or act—on either the camera in the pen tucked in his pocket, nor on the camera that CI Wright had taped to the inside of his back collar. He hadn't been kidding about getting something, coming and going, for the cameras clearly caught all actions being played out, in front and behind Arran. They all knew that any recording captured would be useless in getting a conviction, but they weren't interested in pursuing that avenue, rather were more intent on destroying Rudd's powerbase, beginning with public awareness. After today, it was all of their hope, that their actions would sufficiently yank every tooth from Rudd, Dunne, and all his minions, effectively leaving them harmless—kind of like the abominable snow monster in the old movie classic, Rudolph the Red-nosed Reindeer.

CHAPTER FORTY-TWO

"My heart is hurting," Barbara whispered as they gathered around the mobile phone and watched the two cameras, recording everything going on in Rudd Tower, in Arran's vicinity.

"Do you want to sit down, Sweetheart?" Tim asked. "There isn't reason why you should be watching this."

"Nothing much happening right now to be worried over," Wright interjected, "and if Arran doesn't stop tap-dancing around and get to the root of things, we aren't likely to get any leverage at all."

"Be patient, Chief Inspector," Alastair whispered, watching his brother precede Dunne onto the elevator. "Arran knows that he can't just come out and accuse these men of anything. If he doesn't play their game, act as if he's willing to forget and get back to work, they'll kill him immediately."

"Oh dear…" Barbara cried out, and then moved to the other car, her husband following along behind.

"Apologize for me, will you?" Alastair called out to Tim. "It isn't my intent to cause her anguish."

Tim nodded and then moved to help his wife into their car, "Lie down on the back seat. There's nothing that's going on that you need to bear witness to."

"Please tell me he'll be all right, Timothy," Barbara pleaded softly. She was a strong woman who'd borne heavy loads in her life, but seeing her son walk into the very jaws of evil was threatening to undo her at her core. Attacks on her person she could handle, an attack against her son…she lay down as her husband instructed and breathed deeply, attempting to hold off the tears that threatened.

"I know that we all are going to do everything within our power to ensure that nothing happens to our boy. Now rest. You're going to need to go into mother bear mode soon, and will need all of your strength. Remember, Arran is counting on us."

Barbara closed her eyes and nodded, "I'll be ready, but I can't watch. When it's time to go in, you just point me in the right direction."

"You bet I will," Tim grinned. "Now do as I say and rest. I'm just going to leave the door open, so you get fresh air." He turned and made his way over to where Alastair and CI Wright were intently watching the screen, "Anything?"

"They're still in the elevator. We're hoping to catch a glimpse of which floor it stops on, so we'll know where to go when we're needed," Alastair replied.

"That doesn't look like a standard elevator," Tim observed.

"We think it's either a freight elevator or a dedicated elevator, meant for personnel only," CI Wright replied, "which means it may not have a digital floor display."

"Did we think to look at where they entered from?" Tim asked. "Just in case it doesn't? It may only have one destination…"

"Or several," CI Wright interrupted. "Just because it may be for special use, doesn't mean it has only one stopping point."

"So, we need Arran to think about that and try to inform us so we aren't going in blind," Tim added.

"Or too late," Alastair finished.

"I have to say, I'm looking forward to wiping that smirk off that big oaf's face." Tim snapped, the rear camera catching every sneering moment of Dunne's countenance, as he stood behind Arran in the elevator.

"My biggest concern, aside from Arran's safety," DS Wright said, watching the images flicker, "is whether we'll maintain a signal. The further they descend, the less chance we'll remain connected. If they go much lower, all of this could be for naught."

"Unless we all do what we originally intended—storm the facility en masse, but with mobile phone recorders going. That way, we prevent harm from coming to Arran, possibly get Melissa to safety, and still manage to collect damning footage," Alastair supplied, confidently.

"Well, let's hope we don't lose the signal. Dunne has already provided some incriminating information, but I'd love to capture whatever is in the area they're descending to, as soon as those doors slide open. If we lose the signal and head in, they may have the chance to dispose of any evidence before we can get down there to record anything else. I still think this is our best chance, so keep your fingers crossed."

After another minute, the three watching the mobile monitor observed as Arran turned to face Dunne.

CHAPTER FORTY-THREE

"What do you want, mate?" Dunne asked, and once more Arran found himself improvising.

"I just don't want to face what's waiting, quite frankly," Arran replied forthrightly. "I have to admit, B-4 is not my favorite place to go in Rudd Tower," he quipped, his tone filled with acid, much as the vials filling the cupboard down below.

"With good reason, yeah?" Dunne laughed. "I wouldn't want to be having a meeting with Mr. Rudd down here either. If I was you, I'd be thinking of all kinds of ways to make amends, so he isn't asking me to end you in a very unpleasant way. Still, since you were kind enough to return to the fold, and we managed to prevent DS Lloyd from catching her flight back to England, Mr. Rudd may be in a more forgiving mood," Dunne continued bluntly, no longer concerned about ears listening, since the lower basement was off limits to anyone visiting Rudd Tower, yet swept daily for listening devices, in the event someone did manage to get down there. He couldn't know that Arran was in possession of two recording devices, because he also arrogantly believed that no one who took the trip while in his custody would ever dare attempt to wear a recording device. He was solely reliant upon his intimidating nature, and the threat of what happened to those who crossed Mr. Rudd.

"Is this where you brought Melissa?" Arran asked, dreading the reply.

"I guess to get the answer to that question, you'll need to face the doors, don't you think?" Dunne replied smugly as the elevator came to a halt and the doors slid open. When Arran remained firmly planted, Dunne forcibly turned him about, "Off you go," he said, shoving him out of the elevator.

Arran's gaze immediately located the woman sitting in the chair, and his heart skipped several beats, "Melissa," he whispered.

He snapped out of his daze and raced over to Melissa's side. He lifted her limp head in his hands, and knew instantly that she'd not survived Dunne's torture.

"You son-of-a-bitch!" He screamed, all the pent-up rage he'd held in, resulting from Jane's death, and now Melissa's, erupted, and he barreled at Dunne with all the force of a raging bull.

CHAPTER FORTY-FOUR

"I'd say we've gotten more than enough…" CI Wright began, but the other three were already running to jump in their vehicles. One of the rental cars started up before CI Wright even fully registered they were on the move. Alastair was starting the other rental, when Wright ran around and jumped into the passenger side.

Both cars peeled out across the back lot and were at the front of Rudd Tower within a minute. No one bothered to turn off their ignitions, simply jumped out and headed straight inside.

"Mrs. Masters, you stay here. Wait for police backup. Let them know where we went. Level B4," CI Wright commanded as the three men boarded the elevator. He then pulled out his mobile and dialed 000[6].

What's your emergency?

"This is Chief Inspector Damian Wright. There's been a death at Rudd Tower. I need police backup immediately." He disconnected as soon as he relayed the information, not needing to focus on an operator's questions. "Hopefully, they'll comprehend what I said, and send backup. I only wish one of us was armed."

"Four of us may stand a chance of at least keeping that giant goon busy until those who *are* armed arrive; unless they ignore the call because of the location," Tim Masters snarled. "If they are in Rudd's pocket, as you all suspect, they may just assume that Rudd will handle it in house."

"Well, after today, we're going to give Mr. Rudd and the police department, something to think about," Alastair replied, angrily.

"We can only hope," Tim responded.

The elevator ground to a halt, and the doors slid open to reveal a scene that had each man gaping in horror.

---

[6] 000 is the emergency number for cell phone users in Australia

CHAPTER FORTY-FIVE

Arran barreled into Lachlan Dunne with the force of a steamroller. At least that's what it felt like to Arran. To Dunne, at six feet four inches tall and nearing three hundred pounds, the impact was more akin to a child's motorized play car. He shoved Arran aside and quickly slid a knife from its sheath attached to his belt buckle.

"Let's go," he taunted at Arran who was too furious to notice that Dunne was now armed.

Arran screamed and scrambled to his feet, then rushed at Dunne again. The sound of warning cries reached his ears, but it came too late to prevent him running directly into Dunne's blade.

He doubled over as the blade penetrated his abdomen. The two men remained locked in that position for what seemed interminable, but then Tim snapped out of his daze and launched himself at Dunne.

Tim was comparable in height to Dunne, but age had withered his body and weakened his strength. Still, his angry assault was enough to jar Dunne sideways, which knocked the knife free from his grip, although it remained lodged in Arran's gut. Arran fell to his knees and then tilted over onto his side.

"Get up to the ground floor, and call in a paramedic," CI Wright snapped at Alastair, who stood in indecision for only a moment before retracing his steps hurriedly. He hit the up button, then pulled out Arran's mobile phone from his pocket and dialed *000*. There was no signal. As the elevator climbed, he whispered words of prayer that Arran would be okay until help arrived.

CI Wright raced over and knelt by Arran's side, then pulled a handkerchief from his pocket, "I know it hurts, but try not to touch the hilt. We need Dunne's prints for evidence. I'm sorry." He laid the handkerchief over the hilt in the event that Arran couldn't resist the impulse. "I need to go help your dad," he said compassionately, then stood and ran over to Dunne, ramming his shoulder into the man's back. It knocked him forward into Tim, who lost his balance and swayed backward. After the punch he took to the jaw, staying upright wasn't going to happen.

He fell backward and groaned as his aging tailbone impacted the concrete flooring, but he wrapped a shield of determination about himself and scrambled to his feet, just as CI Wright decked Dunne in the jaw with a right cross.

Dunne staggered, but the size of the man made him more impervious to attacks by men wielding far less strength. Tim knew, from his experience in the armed services, that to take down a combatant bigger in size meant using tactical advantages; striking where the larger man was most vulnerable. Often this meant landing powerful blows in either the knee caps or between the legs. Both of which would topple this Goliath.

CI Wright took a strike to the jaw and fell to the ground, shaking his head to clear the stars circling. He drew in a deep breath and climbed to his feet. He was breathing heavily. Too many years behind a desk and too many beer in his belly had left him soft and incapable of taking on a beefy militant. Still, he knew the idea, at this point, was simply to keep Dunne preoccupied until help arrived.

He swayed slightly when he started toward Dunne again and had to stop until his head ceased swimming. Tim skirted over next to him and placed a restraining hand on his arm, "We can't beat him, even together," he murmured close to Wright's ear, "so we have to cripple him."

"If we can't…"

"Strike a blow at his knees or his groin," Tim explained quickly. "It's the only way to stop him in his tracks."

Dunne stood against the far wall watching the two with a mixture of wariness and fury. It galled him that these laughable excuses for men had gotten the jump on him and managed to disarm him. For that, he was going to make them suffer plenty.

He pushed away from the wall, preparing to charge them, when the elevator door slid open again.

CHAPTER FORTY-SIX

"Why don't we call a stop to this nonsense?" Amherst Rudd called loudly, dangerously, pushing Barbara Masters and Alastair from the elevator ahead of him, a gun trained on their backs, then turned his attention to his enforcer. "I'm more than a little annoyed, Lachlan, over how you allowed things to get this far gone."

Dunne wanted to counter the accusation, but knew that anything he said would be perceived as an excuse. Instead he squared his shoulders and made his way over to his boss' side, "What'll we do with them all," he asked, deflecting attention away from his own failings. "They've likely called the police…"

"Of which I am in charge, you dolt!" Rudd snapped.

CI Wright saw Barbara kneel at her son's side, tears streaming quietly down her cheeks. She reached for the knife. Wright sidled over quickly and knelt down beside her. Pulling her hand away, he whispered in her ear, "Don't touch, or draw attention to the knife, we need it as evidence."

Barbara cried out softly and did her best to contain the tears that threatened to turn into full out sobs.

"Barbara, be strong," Alastair whispered, kneeling on the other side of her. "We're doing everything we can to get out of here. I was able to contact the police again and asked they dispatch an ambulance, before Rudd waylaid you and me, so I know that help must be on the way."

Rudd saw the gathering around the man on the floor and looked back at Dunne, "That isn't my accountant, is it?" He asked, then moved his gaze from Arran to Alastair. "I can't discern the difference between the two."

"We were going to kill him anyway, yeah?" Dunne queried quietly. He'd made so many mistakes the last couple of days that he was more and more worried that he'd be on the receiving end of Rudd's wrath, if he didn't find a way to regain control—both of the current circumstances and the sudden fear wracking his body.

Arran lie as still as he was able and closed his eyes, the pain in his abdomen a fire spreading out to all of his limbs. He tried desperately to keep his breathing even, to keep the pain contained, but he was losing the battle. Consciousness was also something he held on to with sheer strength of will. He refused to pass out because he needed to know his family was going to be ok, and knew that he'd never know what happened to them if he didn't remain lucid.

"And that one over there? Is that the police officer from Leeds?" Rudd asked, waving his gun toward the chair against the far wall.

Dunne nodded.

"Is she dead?"

Dunne nodded again.

Rudd sighed heavily, "Did we at least glean anything of value before you killed her?"

Dunne could not hide the look of embarrassment acknowledging yet another blunder he'd made, and Rudd shook his head in agitated disgust.

Alastair stood and looked toward the wall indicated by Rudd. Everyone had been distracted by the fracas going on from the moment they'd entered the room that none had noticed the lone figure strapped to the chair at the back, partly in shadow. They all *knew* she was there, but in her silence she went unseen.

Alastair shook the shock from his system and made his way over to Melissa's side. He could tell she'd been taken from the world and tears welled in his eyes. Here was another woman who'd died in an attempt to protect Arran—and then himself—two brothers who hadn't even known of each other's existence until a week ago.

"Did you have to kill her?" He screamed at Dunne.

CI Wright also appeared to have just noticed his officer seated strapped to the chair and felt his own ire rise. He knew it was an act in futility, but he pulled his badge from his breast pocket and aimed it at Rudd and Dunne, "That, you sons-of-bitches, was one of my best detective sergeants. A fine officer, and worthy of more respect than you two bottom feeders will ever command; and since you want answers, I'll give them to you, so listen carefully—you're through! Your days are numbered, because no matter what you think you're going to get away with down here today, the word is out. There's no more slithering away into the dark and hiding, no more paying off officers to carry out your dirty work, no more acid baths to silence your opposition. The word is out, do you hear? Everyone knows who you are, what you do, and how you stay in power; so prepare to have the rug yanked from beneath your feet, because today is your day of reckoning."

Rudd and Dunne stood listening, jaws clenching, then Rudd lifted his firearm and shot CI Wright in the chest. He buckled to his knees and was dead within seconds.

Barbara let out a scream and fought to hang on to her own consciousness. She'd been alive for over sixty years and never once had she witnessed such brutality in her life, especially on this level and so near. Tim rushed over to her side and knelt beside her, pulling her into his embrace. She lay her head on his shoulder and started weeping. Alastair moved toward them and knelt beside Barbara, placing a hand in comfort on her shoulder. It was just the four of them now; and not one had police training, nor the ability to fight against the evil standing before them. All they had remaining was the hope that someone would arrive soon, and prevent Rudd from killing any more of their numbers.

"Get the vat," Rudd commanded and Dunne raced off through one of the side doors. When he returned, pushing on a wheeled flatbed dolly, an enormous tub formed from a Polymethylpentene material, he didn't need any further instructions—it was time to dispose of both the witnesses and the incriminating evidence. He'd done this so many times in the years he'd worked for Rudd that he didn't even blink anymore; it didn't faze him that he was eradicating an entire human being from existence, just never so many at once.

"Work quickly," Rudd instructed. "We can keep this quiet as long as there isn't any explaining to do."

"I thought you didn't have to worry about the police, Rudd," Alastair spat. "Thought you had them all in your pocket."

"Yeah, well, ignorance of my activities has helped in that regard," Rudd admitted. "No witnesses doesn't hurt either."

"There's still the commentary that was released in the morning edition. You can't undo that," Alastair taunted. "We made certain that everyone knows what sort of man you are; the threats you made to our lives, the harm you caused Arran; linking you to the deaths of Arran's fiancé and another reporter. And now there's a recording of the death of DS Lloyd that will be distributed soon also. You aren't going to be able to hide from it, even if you dispose of us all."

"No, but without you to corroborate those accounts, it'll be given as much weight as fairy stories, and soon forgotten," Rudd goaded in return. "As for the editor of that paper that allowed that commentary to be printed…well, let's just say, he'll be regretting that decision shortly, and since none of you will be alive to distribute any video footage…well, I'll not be concerning myself over it." Rudd turned his attention to Dunne who was busily setting up the hoist mechanism, "I'll keep the police at bay and get them out of here quickly. You just make certain that when I return, there isn't anyone left to do any lip flapping. You'll need my gun to ensure that none of them flail about too much when you lower them in the acid. Don't want a repeat of that one man you tried to dunk alive. Nasty business that. A lot of acidic pits in my concrete that needed filling. It's fully loaded, minus the one bullet, so make certain you use it. You'll not be able to restrain them all otherwise." He held the gun out, and Dunne raced over to collect it. "I'm off. Don't fail me again."

Rudd backed into the elevator and as the door slid closed, he heard the first shot fired.

CHAPTER FORTY-SEVEN

Dunne walked over, closer to the group huddled together in the center of the room, took aim, and fired a bullet into Arran's head, "There, out of his misery now," he stated flatly over the top of Barbara's wails and the outraged screams of Tim and Alastair.

"You sadistic son-of-a-bitch!" Tim screamed. "My son had a chance…"

"No, he didn't," Dunne antagonized. "You didn't really think we'd let a paramedic down here, did you? Best he die quick anyway. Did him a favor. Now he's done suffering."

"I'll show you suffering," Tim muttered, nearly unintelligible, as Dunne waved the gun about taunting them as to who would get the next bullet.

Alastair stood slowly and squared his shoulders, "If you're going to do this, best be to it. Your boss did say to make it quick, and provoking us isn't precisely following his directives." He didn't particularly want to die, but neither did he care to have this man making their last moments on earth a living hell either. He'd already done severe damage to Tim and Barbara Masters by taking away their only son; he couldn't see how it was doing them much good to suffer further. What he didn't anticipate was that Tim Masters would use his distraction to make his move.

The elderly man pushed aside his age-associated aches and pains and swift as an adder, launched himself sideways from his seated position, striking hard into Dunne's knees. The tall man grunted loudly, as one of his knees popped out of joint and he fell hard on his side, his shoulder striking the concrete surface, jolting the gun from his hand.

Alastair bent and retrieved the weapon and pointed it at Dunne. He'd never fired a gun, never taken a life, but he was having difficulty with not doing so at this moment. He had just decided he could pull the trigger when Tim leapt to his feet and began kicking hard at Dunne's back. The hitman arched in pain, and tried to scurry away, but each time he tried to slither off, Tim would land another kick.

"Tim, step aside," Alastair said emotionless. "I'll take care of this now. Go untie Melissa. We can't leave her body here. We'll need to decide how to get her, Arran, and CI Wright in the elevator."

"I say we shoot this bastard in the head and dunk his body in that vat over there," Tim spat, as he moved to release Melissa from her bindings. "Give him what he was about to give us," he continued, carefully hefting her limp body and then placing it on the ground next to his son.

"And I couldn't agree more," Alastair concurred, "but whatever we decide to do, it needs to be quick. We need to get up that elevator before the police leave. We won't get another chance to make Rudd pay for these deaths. Barbara, I know you are having a difficult time, but I need you to locate CI Wright's phone. We're going to need that footage he recorded. Can you do that?"

Barbara sniffed loudly, swiping at the tears that wouldn't stop falling. She nodded stiffly, but couldn't find the words to speak past the lump in her throat and the pain in her heart. She winced in embarrassed discomfort several times as she began rooting through Wrights pockets.

"Tim, I hate to ask this of you, but we really need that knife too…" he started, then caught a movement from the corner of his eye. For the first time in his life, he fired a gun.

CHAPTER FORTY-EIGHT

"I'm telling you, it was a hoax," Rudd asserted to Staff Superintendent Turner, who'd answered the emergency call to Rudd Tower personally—along with Inspector Massey and a half dozen other officers. "What name did the caller give again?"

"Chief Inspector Wright," Turner replied, his tone stern.

"And we both know there isn't any such person within the Perth Police…"

"He's DS Lloyd's superior officer from Leeds, England," Turner interrupted. "I know this because he called me yesterday and asked if I'd received an email outlining some fairly disturbing information about you, Mr. Rudd, and your associate, Lachlan Dunne."

"Well, whoever made that prank emergency call must have just pulled that name out of a hat, because there isn't anything untoward going on here," Rudd emphasized more firmly, unused to being questioned by anyone. "Now I suggest you return to your offices and be just as attentive to genuine emergency calls."

"Mr. Rudd," Turner began, refusing to relent, "are you aware of information that was printed in the newspaper this morning? The emergency call from here on the heels of that article and upon the heels of the phone call from CI Wright yesterday is a bit too much for me to overlook as coincidental."

Mr. Rudd's face reddened in anger. Not only had the six people in his subbasement, separately or as a whole, caused him no end in grief the last couple of days, but their actions continued to even after their deaths. He didn't like the feelings of unraveling that gripped his nerves of late, "I am aware that there was an attempt to slander my good name, yes, and I hope that you'll be the one to deal with that editor personally and decisively for allowing that tripe to be printed."

"I would love to speak to him about it, yes; however, when I received word of a shooting here at Rudd Tower, I decided that too many happenstances were leading to trouble, so had an officer go by the paper to pick up the editor. I was told that a rather intimidating fellow escorted a petrified, pasty-faced Oliver Carter from his offices about an hour ago. His wife hasn't heard from him since."

"I wouldn't know anything about that," Rudd declared.

"There doesn't appear too much you are aware of related to all of these accusations leveled at you," Turner replied. "But as we do take all emergency calls very seriously, and this caller happened to mention a death on these premises, we are obligated to investigate."

"You, Superintendent, are making a grave error in judgement," Rudd whispered threateningly.

Turner blanched, but he was tired of Rudd playing puppeteer to him and his men, so if he could finally locate tangible evidence of foul play—something no other had been able to do prior to today— then hopefully he could yank loose the strings binding him and his men, once and for all. If he didn't…well, he knew that he was putting himself and his family in Rudd's direct line of fire. He had to find something. "Men, spread out. Cover every inch of Rudd Tower. If there's been a death here, I want that body discovered," he called out, then added as a measure of security for his and his men's safety, "we need to put Mr. Rudd's mind at ease that there isn't a lunatic going about his offices injuring people."

"I still think you're making a grave error in judgement, despite your sudden concern over my safety," Rudd stated sarcastically.

"Well, as you said, if this did happen to be a prank call, then we'll turn up nothing and be out of your building shortly," Turner replied. Just as he turned to aid in the search, the elevator doors, from the far side of the foyer, slid open.

"Massey, cover him," Turner yelled, then ran toward the elevator.

CHAPTER FORTY-NINE

"Get out!" Alastair said sternly, pressing the gun against Dunne's back. "And don't you dare drop Arran's body," he added, his tone more menacing than he realized he was capable of sounding. Dunne limped out, his foot on fire where Alastair shot him; added to that the pain in his back, and Alastair had reason to be concerned he'd drop the body. He was barely able to hold himself upright.

Just as they exited the elevator, a man came racing up to them, "What in bloody hell happened here?"

"We need the police, please," Barbara whispered, her tone thick with emotion.

"Ma'am, I am the police. Someone explain what's going on? Are these people okay? Do I need to contact emergency services..."

"They're dead," Tim said harshly, "killed by this man," he snapped, indicating Dunne with the tilt of his head.

"On order of Mr. Amherst Rudd," Alastair added, "who personally shot CI Wright, whose still lying in the elevator."

Turner's jaw dropped and he found himself speechless.

Alastair pushed the gun harder into Dunne's back, "Lay my brother down, and be careful about it," he ordered, "then go back in to get CI Wright's body and place it beside his. Tim, why don't you carefully place Melissa beside Arran?"

He watched, stunned, as Dunne turned and hefted Wright from the elevator car then shuffled to where he'd placed Arran. He lowered Wright down beside the two others and then stood, his face as emotionless as a stone slab.

Seeing the bodies, lying side-by-side, finally shook Turner from his shock and he looked up at the battered face of Rudd's henchman, "I think I need answers, but first...Lachlan Dunne, I'm placing you under arrest for the murders of..." he paused and looked at Alastair.

"Arrans Masters, Detective Sergeant Melissa Lloyd, and Chief Inspector Wright of the Leeds Police Department," Alastair filled in for him.

"Right," Turner said, then pulled his handcuffs from his back pocket. As he shackled Dunne, he yelled at Massey, "Cuff Rudd!"

"You'll do no such thing!" Rudd screamed back, and started backing toward the staircase. "I'll not be held accountable for the rogue actions of one of my men."

"Very well, Mr. Rudd, I'll not cuff you," Massey said soothingly, "but it would help our investigation a great deal if you'd be willing to come down to answer questions about why you think your hireling went rogue, as you say."

"That I'd be willing to do," Rudd replied, lifting his chin haughtily. "I've done nothing, and you'll never be able to prove otherwise," he said, his tone superior.

"I'm sure we'll clear this mess up before morning, sir," Massey said, leading Rudd out of the building and to his patrol car.

Turner came out next, shoving a quiet, compliant Dunne into the second patrol car. As soon as he was free of his prisoner he turned to Massey, "What was that pussy-footing around Rudd all about?" He asked, his tone agitated, worried that Rudd's hold was still gripping his officers.

"Just needed him to come out without more bloodshed, sir," Massey stated.

Turner nodded, "Good thinking…well, I need you to stay behind to see that those three bodies in there get escorted to the medical examiner unimpeded. And I want you to stand guard until I get the autopsy report."

"Sir?"

"You and I both know that Rudd could have more people on his payroll than we're aware. Once word gets out that we've got him in custody…well, we don't want bodies to go missing or those reports. Also, you're to ensure that the medical examiner understands that those three take priority, and if he has an issue with that, have him call me on my personal mobile. When it's done, get that paperwork to me, and me alone."

Massey pulled a pen and notepad from his pocket, "Your number, sir?" Turner called it off and Massey jotted it down, "I'll see to it, sir."

"You and I are done, right, Massey?"

"Done, sir?"

"Done being threatened into working for that…"

"Oh…one hundred percent, sir. I couldn't be more relieved that we're finally done."

"SS Turner, sir!" An officer, obviously flustered, came racing over to where he and Massey stood. "I just received word that they've located that editor…"

"Oliver Carter?" Turner supplied.

"Correct sir…"

"Good, we'll need his added testimony."

"No, sir. That is…well, sir…they found his body in Swan River, sir."

Turner sucked in a huge breath, then let it out in a whoosh, "This is beyond heinous. So much death," he muttered. "Massey, ensure that Carter's corpse gets on that list of priority autopsies. We're going to need all the ammunition we can get, if we're going to bring down Rudd."

"I will, sir, but the way things are going," Massey replied softly, "all the evidence is pointing to Lachlan Dunne being the murderer. How are we going to tie Rudd to any of it, if he never gets his hands dirty?"

"Oh, he may not have pulled the trigger on every person who's died, but he's definitely the one giving the orders, and he was fingered as shooting a police officer, so I promise you that I'll do all I can to get him on more than accessory to commit murder. He's going down for at least one murder, and as an accomplice in this as sure as if he pulled the trigger on the others. Handing Dunne that gun makes him an accomplice."

His focus shifted to Barbara, Tim, and Alastair being escorted from the building which interrupted his tirade, "I need to see to these three living witnesses," he muttered tiredly to Massey. "You get to the morgue." He walked over to meet the three maltreated survivors, "Do any of you need medical assistance before we begin your statements?" He asked.

All three shook their heads.

"Very good. You all can ride to the station with me."

"Sir?" Alastair said, his tone weary. "You'll need this. This is what got everyone killed; it's what started it all." He pulled out an item wrapped in a handkerchief and handed it to Turner. "It should have Dunne's prints on it."

Turner opened the handkerchief and stared for a moment at the blood-soaked blade, then looked back at Alastair, "I thought people were shot."

"Not everyone, but all of this destruction didn't start today—with a gun. It began when Rudd sent Lachlan Dunne onto British soil to kill a reporter named Jane Chaffin—my twin brother's fiancé. If you take a mold of that blade and send it to the medical examiner in Leeds, I'm as certain as can be that it'll be a match. DS Lloyd came here to get that knife; to get proof of Dunne's guilt, but just as important, we wanted justice for Jane."

"And you'll have it—along with justice for your brother, DS Lloyd, CI Wright, and Oliver Carter."

"Oliver's dead also?" Alastair said, his body deflating even further.

"I'm afraid so, yes. They're fishing his body out of the Swan River. Printing that commentary from all of you in the morning edition pretty much ensured he wouldn't survive the day."

"Yet he did it willingly—for Jane—for all of them," Alastair whispered, tears streaming down his cheeks. The loss of so many was beginning to sink in, and he sank to his knees.

Turner knelt beside him, "I'll find a way to charge them both with so many atrocious crimes, that Australia's government may just be inclined to temporarily reinstate capital punishment."

"That man took our son," Tim whispered harshly, "so if they need someone to flip the switch on those two, you just give me a call."

"No," Barbara whispered, placing a hand on Alastair's head. "I say it should be an eye for an eye, like the Good Book says. Let them see what it's like to have their bodies eaten away with acid."

Alastair looked up into Barbara's pain-stricken gaze and felt his heart crush even further. He pushed himself up from his knees and wrapped his arms around her, "We can't let them steal our humanity," he whispered. "We have to be better than they are."

"That's not so easy when you've lost so much," Tim replied hoarsely.

Alastair nodded, "I know, but you still have each other, and that's a starting point for healing."

"And we have you too," Barbara said softly, wrapping her arms tightly about Alastair's waist.

"I can't replace Arran," he whispered, pained.

"No, but you were twins," Tim said, his tone thick with tears, "and that makes you just as much our son as he was. It'll help us all, I think, to get past the pain we're all in, if you'll see fit to…."

Alastair nodded, "Dad, Mom…let's go see justice done."

"For Arran and Jane," Barbara added.

"CI Wright and Oliver Carter," Tim continued.

"And all of those who fell victim to a brutal tycoon whose total disregard for humanity took away loved ones from more people than we'll ever know."

www.ingramcontent.com/pod-product-compliance
Lightning Source LLC
Chambersburg PA
CBHW011509100726
47900CB00009B/2659